'I never expla

'You will,' Adam
just a hint of mc
amusement was infuriating.

Yvonne's reaction was the instant detonation of heat-lightning. She flashed, 'I'll not be put on a leash, damn you!'

'No?' That as a question, with those dark eyebrows slanting upwards, was salt rubbed into the wound. 'Perhaps you should be, then.'

Dear Reader

As Easter approaches, Mills & Boon are delighted to present you with an exciting selection of sixteen new titles. Why not take a trip to our Euromance locations—Switzerland or western Crete, where romance is celebrated in great style! Or maybe you'd care to dip into the story of a family feud or a rekindled love affair? Whatever tickles your fancy, you can always count on love being in the air with Mills & Boon!

The Editor

Amanda Carpenter was raised in South Bend, Indiana but lived for many years in England. She started writing because she felt a need to communicate with people from other walks of life. She wrote her first romance novel when she was nineteen and has been translated into many languages. Although she has many interests including music and art, writing is her greatest love.

THE WINTER KING

BY

AMANDA CARPENTER

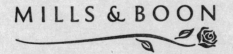

MILLS & BOON

MILLS & BOON LIMITED
ETON HOUSE, 18-24 PARADISE ROAD
RICHMOND, SURREY TW9 1SR

All the characters in this book have no existence outside the imagination of the Author, and have no relation whatsoever to anyone bearing the same name or names. They are not even distantly inspired by any individual known or unknown to the Author, and all the incidents are pure invention.

All Rights Reserved. The text of this publication or any part thereof may not be reproduced or transmitted in any form or by any means, electronic or mechanical, including photocopying, recording, storage in an information retrieval system, or otherwise, without the written permission of the publisher.

This book is sold subject to the condition that it shall not, by way of trade or otherwise, be lent, resold, hired out or otherwise circulated without the prior consent of the publisher in any form of binding or cover other than that in which it is published and without a similar condition including this condition being imposed on the subsequent purchaser.

*First published in Great Britain 1994
by Mills & Boon Limited*

© Amanda Carpenter 1994

*Australian copyright 1994
Philippine copyright 1994
This edition 1994*

ISBN 0 263 78454 1

*Set in Times Roman 10 on 12 pt.
01-9404-52343 C*

Made and printed in Great Britain

PROLOGUE

SHE was a scion of Hollywood's tinsel aristocracy. Her late grandmother had been a legendary movie queen, her grandfather one of the film industry's most powerful moguls. Her mother and father carried on the tradition: their combined efforts totalled four Oscars and five nominations.

When she was six, she was on the cover of *Vogue* and *Harper* magazines with her mother. By the time she was ten she was an internationally famous child model. By sixteen, because of her parents' careful orchestration of her career and wise investments, she was independently wealthy.

At seventeen she left the modelling profession and acted in her first film. At nineteen she abandoned her excellent tutors. By twenty-one she had become one of the top five movie box-office draws in the world, had earned an Oscar of her own, and had been featured on the cover of *Time* magazine. She had met two presidents, queens and kings and princes, and had been courted by a desert sheikh.

One morning, after attending the Cannes international film festival, she stood at the edge of the Mediterranean Sea. She had starred in a total of eight films. Three had been in the last year alone, all of which had been filmed on location: Mexico, London, Monte Carlo, the Canary Islands, Cairo and Morocco.

As she stood with her bare feet in the warm silken waters, her famous, unforgettable face was to the sea, and the French city of Nice at her back.

She was twenty-two years old, and frightened.

She couldn't remember which country she was in.

She had been Celeste, Mary, Elizabeth, Eloise, Rhiannon, Sara, Diane and Isabella.

She couldn't remember her own name.

'I quit,' she heard herself say to the blank cerulean sky, and knew it to be true. Then, as far as the outside world was concerned, she disappeared, and remained a mystery for two years.

CHAPTER ONE

ANGER was good.

The Porsche growled into Beverly Hills, sleek and low-slung and anonymous in the extravagant setting. California had suffered drought in the last five years, but the evidence of the natural calamity stopped at the outskirts of fairyland, where the intrusion of reality was strongly discouraged.

She liked the emotion anger; it was clean and strong and vitalising. Definitive. She savoured her fury, fuelled it, pampered it, with the expertise of the connoisseur. She didn't know anybody who could sustain anger as long and as effectively as she could; maybe it was a record or something, a mark of some distinction. She had gone past the point of needing distinguishing marks, tattoos on the soul, psychic dental plates, but she hadn't given up the habit of looking for them.

The Porsche pulled to a stop before high security gates. She didn't bother calling the house, instead punching the computer code that would allow her entrance into the lavish fortress. When the gates swung open she drove through fast, roared up the long, manicured driveway, manoeuvred past a kaleidoscopic army of luxury cars, limousines and chauffeurs, and slewed to a precipitate stop around the side of the house.

The mansion was ablaze with lights, music and hordes of people. How fashionable. She was late.

She left the keys and her luggage in the car and strode up to the front doors. The maid who answered and looked up at her was transformed with delight in an instant. 'Oh, Miss Trent!'

'Hello, Betty,' she said, as mildly as if she had gone for an afternoon stroll and her two-year absence had never been. 'My luggage is in the Porsche around the side. See to it, will you?'

She left the maid gabbling. People were everywhere, in the massive hall, the reception-rooms, up the stairs. In dinner-jackets and evening gowns, torn jeans, furs and feathers, jewelled, coiffed and perfumed, and painted, everyone was a study of attitude, punctuated with uniformed house staff and caterers: actors, agents, writers, producers, politicians and businessmen, wives and mistresses, models and artists, and bohemian hangers-on.

She prowled through the mansion, a panther on the hunt, not oblivious to the ripple of effect her presence had on the crowd, but uncaring. People turned, stared at her in amazed excitement, and gossip and speculation ran in her wake like wildfire.

The occupants in the main reception having been searched and discarded, she turned her attention towards the back reception, a great marbled hall with open veranda doors leading to the sumptuous gardens and swimming-pool. A rock group blared in one corner.

She strolled to the middle of the crowded floor and stopped, a clawed and sinuous predator among the peacocks.

She was patient in the pursuit, and methodical. She would tear Hollywood apart if she had to, but she had been promised he would be present tonight, and so she searched the crowd as a general surveyed a battlefield.

Her mother Vivian, petite and immaculately feminine in a Dior creation, was flirting with a greying man in one corner. Her father Christopher was dancing, a tall and distinguished man who appeared to be enjoying himself without a care in the world. They were a family of actors.

Her brother David would be around somewhere. Her parents had not yet seen her, but they would soon. She noted their positions and dismissed them, and then her gaze lit on the object of her search. She recognised the object from the Press photographs that had accompanied the various articles written about him over the years.

There.

Adam Ruarke was a tall, slim man, elegantly and gracefully moulded. His dark auburn hair shone wine-red, his skin a light gold by comparison. His erect carriage, the length of his bone-structure, the tensile male handsomeness of that spare carved face, were masterpieces of design. One might be forgiven, in the face of such terrible beauty, for hoping his eyes did not live up to their legend.

One would be disappointed, for his dark-lashed eyes lifted and they were as chill and as grey as an Arctic snowstorm, housing a stunning intelligence. The winter king had knocked at the gates of the land of perpetual summer, and had been invited in.

Adam Ruarke was an inventory in brilliance. At thirty-five the Scottish film director dominated the industry. An ex-Shakespearian actor, he had taken the director's chair eight years ago. For the last five years his every film had reigned supreme against the competition, sweeping the most awards, achieving both critical acclaim and immense popular success. He redefined genres and broke new ground, and jaded Hollywood bowed down to him in awe.

She knew the fabled Iceman by reputation. They had never met.

She smiled, a tiny violence. They were about to meet now.

Someone had laid a hand on her bare arm and was bleating at her. She shook away the sheep and began to stalk her prey.

Adam Ruarke's ice-storm eyes sparkled as they roamed over the room. The small restlessness was the only evidence that he might have tired of his voluptuous companion. Then his gaze lit on her, and stayed in arrested recognition.

She was a woman of sultry poetry in motion. Her height was sheathed in austere black leather trousers, and gleaming flat-heeled boots, and a plain black camisole top with blade-thin spaghetti straps. Her shapely legs were as slim as a gazelle's, the curve of hip and breast superbly highlighted by the long, slender waist and the exquisite bone-structure of her shoulders and arms.

Her magnificent gleaming chestnut hair sprang from a widow's peak and tumbled to her waist in a neglected windblown tangle. Her face was not beautiful viewed in person: the high cheekbones, the hollows underneath and narrow jaw, the straight nose and wide forehead were a shade too adamantly defined. But the inhuman camera adored such definition, and her full, precisely chiselled mouth and massive velvet dark eyes were perfection.

Her fine skin and body were unadorned with either make-up or jewellery. She looked relentlessly naked in sea of baroque artifice, pared to a keen and flawless essence; her utter lack of concern for her own appearance was a powerful statement in itself.

As his chill grey eyes met hers, she let her rage, so carefully banked and tended over the last two weeks, flare inside into a blinding climax. Ah.

He was straight and hard and shining as the noonday sun, and she came up to eclipse him, a dusky, feline shadow. What a surprise: his slender length topped her five feet eleven inches, and she had to look up.

The winter king was amused. It showed in the line of his elegant mouth.

'Yvonne Trent,' said Adam Ruarke in a musical sardonic tone. 'So at last the prodigal returns.'

Yvonne did not check as she came to stand in front of him. She threw the entire strength of her weight into her arm. Her body was one fluid classical pirouette as she slapped him in the face.

The force of the blow rocked his head back and numbed her to the shoulder. She was an athletic woman. She was frankly amazed it hadn't knocked him down.

The chill beauty of his features had been a pale imitation of the awesome white blaze towering before her now. Silence radiated out a good twenty feet around them, as the crack sounded over the music and conversation: except for a faint, unregarded shriek from his blonde companion. In front of an avid and shark-like audience, she had branded him.

Feral satisfaction gleamed in Yvonne's sharp features and immense dark eyes, as she flexed her hand and wrist. Sufficient unto the day.

Having done what she had come to do, she was already turning away from him on one booted heel, dismissing his existence with the same complete indifference with which she had dismissed everything and everyone else since arriving home. She took just one step.

Her arms were seized from behind. Again she was amazed, at the effortless steel strength in the long, slim fingers that snaked around her wrists and yanked them behind her back. She tried one vicious jerk to gain her freedom, and only succeeded in wrenching her shoulder. He drove her before him, an unbreakable, ravening, elemental force at her back.

Yvonne caught the hasty approach of Vivian and Christopher out of the corner of her eye. Naturally they were appalled, but not amazed; they knew their daughter.

'Hello, Mother, Dad,' said Yvonne almost idly as she was force-marched past her parents. 'How've you been keeping?'

Said the Iceman, to her father, one terse clipped word—'Privacy.'

Christopher Trent hesitated only for a moment. 'Upstairs.'

They strode through the hall. The man behind her steered her like a recalcitrant ship through the people. Her eyes narrowed in thought as she watched the various astonished expressions on their faces go past.

The winter king, apparently, was a mind-reader as well. A silken and menacing voice in her ear said gently, 'Try to scream. I invite you. It would give me an excellent reason for stuffing a gag into your lovely mouth.'

Immensely surprised, she didn't scream. She threw back her head and laughed out loud instead.

If anything, his bruising grip on her arms tightened. Yvonne was nearly running by the time they cleared the top of the stairs. Certainly she was breathing hard, as they strode down the wide corridor, startling one or two people into jumping hastily out of their way.

'No,' she said, when he would have stopped at the first door. She dragged him forward, ignoring the extra strain on her shoulders as he refused to relinquish his hold, until they reached the end of the corridor. Then Yvonne steered left to the last door that was partly ajar, leaned back against the man who held her prisoner, and with one foot she kicked the door open to her old suite of rooms.

The maid Betty, in the process of unpacking her suitcase, nearly leaped out of her skin and whirled to gape at the amazing sight of the pair in the doorway.

Yvonne's body was bowed backwards, one strand of her dishevelled hair slung across her eyes; her bare shoulders rested against the hard white chest of the auburn-haired man behind her, his carved, handsome face searingly alive with such a peculiar expression, as his ferocious grey eyes stared at the woman he held captured in his hands.

They must have appeared as some bizarre kind of partnership, with the shape of her hand reddening the Iceman's taut, lean cheek, and the assertive way she had led him to the door. Yvonne was laughing again like a crazy woman as she read the eloquent expression in the maid's wide eyes.

'Thank you, Betty,' she said. 'That'll be all.'

The maid stared at the sulphurous menace at her back. 'Miss Trent——' stammered the smaller woman, obviously intimidated and yet holding her ground '—are you sure you wouldn't like for me to—that is, I'd be glad to stay and finish——?'

Adam Ruarke's icy gaze met the maid's. 'If I were you,' he purred, 'I would get while the getting is good.'

The maid's defiance lasted all of two seconds. She even closed the door behind her when she bolted. As soon as he heard the tiny sound of the latch clicking into place, the man at her back threw her across the room.

Yvonne landed, with emphatic precision, face-down on the middle of her large bed. She gasped at the jarring impact, her hair floating in a glorious fan about her head and shoulders, then she found purchase with tingling hands, and thrust up.

The winter king had circled her, hawk-like, as she came up on her hands and knees and met his hooded grey stare through the veil of her wild hair. She was panting, in high roaring temper and exhilaration. She appeared to hover on the brink of motion, an undomesticated cat readying either to lunge at his throat or to spring away.

He looked—electrified. She glared, then sat back on her knees to fling away the obstructing mass of her hair. When she looked at him again, he had coiled himself in again: that flawless, legendary self-control of his.

Adam Ruarke leaned against the wall, crossed his arms and kicked one foot over the other. His eyes narrowed; honed to a keening edge, he performed laser surgery on her face. Unknown to her, one of her hands crept to her cheek, to finger the unmarked flesh in wonderment.

'Explain yourself.'

There was no anger in his stern and beautiful face, the cut of that elegant mouth, or his voice. There was no emotion whatsoever. He was perfect in his stillness, like a statue again, but the concept of such a vital male being nothing more than cold stone instead of warm-blooded humanity was an incredible offence. My God, she thought in equal parts of amusement and anger, he must be soulless. She would have to provoke him even further.

He spoke the Queen's English with exquisite richness; Yvonne offered it back to him in perfect mocking mimicry. 'I never explain anything.'

His muscled, tensile gracefulness had become that of a master swordsman, deadly and impassive as he studied his opponent before moving in for the kill.

'You will,' he told her. His mouth quirked, just a hint of movement, but the suggestion of amusement was infuriating, a casual flick of the rapier while those grey eyes watched perpetually.

Her reaction was the instant detonation of heat-lightning. She flashed, 'I'll not be put on a leash, damn you!'

'No?' That as a question, with those dark eyebrows slanting upwards, was salt rubbed into the wound. 'Perhaps you should be, then.'

Her great dark eyes were as blank as her incredible face. She gave him no warning; she gave him nothing. Still he was at the door before her and blocking the exit, even as she exploded from the disturbed bed. She laughed then in the defeat of her second bid for freedom just as she had before, an angry, quiet little aside to herself, as if in the confirmation of the vagaries of men.

'You're making a severe mistake, my friend,' she whispered. His ice did not crack at the warning. 'Consider carefully what you do. I'll make your days a living hell if you don't let me go.'

'How extraordinary,' remarked Adam Ruarke, who—astoundingly—smiled. It was a singularly handsome and unattractive expression. 'And after you went to such extravagant lengths to bring me to your bedroom. I've had a multitude of actresses attempt many different ploys to get my—er—attention, but I must admit, Yvonne Trent, your approach wins the brass ring.'

Her narrow hands curled into claws; her breath whistled high and audible through flared nostrils. She spat, 'Spare me the gratuitous fantasies of a vain and self-deluded man! Incredible as it may be for you to believe, I did not walk away from this industry two years ago just to fall meekly into line at the first hint of your manipulations! You're not the first to have tried to get me back. Get your mind out of your pants and off the casting couch—I quit!'

He looked at her narrow-eyed, as if he'd never seen a specimen such as she before, and he didn't appear to like the experience. 'And you quit with such apparent vehemence,' he murmured.

She nearly smiled. He was getting the message. Good. 'And I'm not coming back either,' she growled.

'Oh, you're wrong,' said Adam Ruarke vividly, as he ran one long hand through the darkling flame of his hair and leaned a shoulder against the door. 'You've already come back, from whatever God-forsaken place you'd hidden yourself in. All the way back from—where?—to me, tonight, just to slap my face and to tell me you've retired? It sounds to me as if you're already on a leash, darling.'

She cocked her head to one side. Time to try another tactic. 'How dare you?' she said quietly, and her eyes were magnetic pools absorbing shadows, dark mirrors to the disillusionment of the soul. She bled for the tragedy of fine ideals destroyed; it shone in her gaze, wet and vulnerable and heartbreakingly fragile. 'How dare you play with my father's career like that? Do you know what you've done to him, holding that part over his head like a weapon? He's a fine and qualified actor who's had the bad luck to play unsuccessful parts in the last few years. They're business mistakes—they don't reflect on his ability.'

The Iceman stared at her, transfixed: were tears really the way to melt him? 'I'm beginning to see for myself what your father's abilities are,' replied Adam Ruarke slowly. 'I know he wants the part, of course. Any self-respecting actor would: as the female lead's dying father, the role isn't a central one, but it's so exquisitely written that it's ripe for an Oscar-winning performance.'

'You've made that part look like his salvation,' she accused, then bowed her slender neck, too tired for bitterness. The tears spilled on to her cheeks. 'And then you withhold it. How can you be so cruel as to make his part contingent on whether I take the lead or not? Can't you see now how wrong you've been? He's perfect for that role—I'm the one who's wrong for your project.'

He started to shake. She peered at him, sidelong through furtive lashes, and ground her teeth in fury at what she saw.

Adam Ruarke, emotionless, soulless, cold-hearted demon that he was, threw back his wine-red head and shouted with laughter. It was deep-throated and full-bellied, a male roar of sheer delight. It carved through her head and heart, and, shaken with complex reaction, all she could do was stand stiffly in the face of it and glare.

'I stand amazed,' said the Iceman when he had recovered enough to speak. 'Yes, I believe I'm quite overcome with it. Young lady, you surpass all my expectations. The tears— God, yes, the tears were just the right touch.'

The tears had dried as if by magic. Yvonne's lips were pulled back in a snarl of rage. Her hands twitched in deep, yearning desire; he saw it, and smiled at her gently, and purred, 'Don't even consider it. You got your one shot at me. You won't get another.'

'How can you be so sure?' she said. Her face was taut as a bowstring humming before the release of an arrow, but her eyes were desperately wary with the sense of an impending trap. 'Unless, of course, you agree with me and have decided not to pursue this any further.'

'But I don't agree with you at all,' replied her tormentor easily, as his grey eyes ravished every nuance in her expression. 'I find I've got a different opinion entirely. You'll take the part of the female lead, your father will get his role, and I—get what I want. A perfectly equitable solution all around.'

'No,' she whispered, her throat tight.

He smiled at her impatiently. 'How can you say that? You haven't even seen the script. It's a beauty of a piece, challenging and evocative and multidimensional—any other actress would give her eye-teeth to get such an opportunity.'

She shook her head and the strands of her chestnut hair whipped through the air. Her arms were crossed around her narrow mid-section. 'You're just not listening to me. I'm not an actress any more,' she whispered.

'Rubbish,' he snapped shortly, his dark brows coming together in a harsh frown. 'You've been acting since the moment you showed up on the doorstep. You do it as naturally as you breathe; you've got so much talent seething inside you, you don't even know what to do with it.'

But where had been her fatal mistake? How had she lost her advantage to come to this débâcle? She'd come to conquer, and he had her on the run, and she was terrified at what he saw and said to her.

Her dark gaze clung to his. She refused to acknowledge it as entreaty, and threatened, 'I won't do it. You can't make me. I'll thwart you at every turn—I'll make you wish you'd never laid eyes on me.'

'Shadows,' said the Iceman dismissively, his icy gaze a caress, his elegant mouth ruthless. 'Spitfire and shadows. You love your father too much for that. Give it up, Yvonne. You came, you're here, you're mine.'

She shivered, then flung her lovely head back proudly. 'You underestimate me.'

'No,' he murmured, shifting his position so that he leaned fully back against the door of her cage, his flame-dark head back against the wood in a deceptive attitude of laziness. 'I'm just getting the measure of you.'

'Your arrogance is beyond endurance,' she flung out wildly, goaded, whirling to stalk to the middle of the floor and stand there bewildered. 'You know nothing of what I am or who I've been, or what I can or cannot do!'

He said, with slow, shattering deliberation, 'Do I not, Celeste?'

Her mouth opened on a silent, stunned gasp.

Adam said, 'Do I not, Mary?'

Her back was to him. She was across the room. Of course he couldn't see the fine tremor that ran through her body; of course he couldn't.

He asked in a tenderly employed relentlessness, 'Do I not, Elizabeth, Eloise, Rhiannon, Sara——?'

She cried out loud, the wordless agony the sound of a falcon shot out of the sky, and the fine tremors broke the regal stance of her body, and she fell to her knees and bowed her shoulders in defeat.

'My God.'

Someone was shaken. Yvonne closed her eyes, spearing inwards for her centre: her centre, not anyone else's, not that loss of identity, not that ever again.

Someone was bending over her, a canopy of protection against the harsh light. In a minute she could take the time to remember the present.

'My dear God.'

Someone stroked the hair away from her ashen face with long, clever fingers, came down to the floor in front of her, slid a steel-muscled arm around her waist, which bent back pliant as a willow tree. In a minute she would understand the relevance of all this, why her head fell back strengthlessly and was cradled in the palm of a single hand, why her twisted bow of a mouth was covered with another's gentle sensuality.

The winter king kissed her in twilight warmth. Her eyes opened; could a face carved in stony remorse be warm? Her fingers flew to answer the question and found it to be so, warm and vibrantly male and every bit as vitalising as anger and even more definitive.

'Yvonne, I'm sorry,' he whispered. 'We went too far. I didn't mean to hurt you like that; I didn't know——'

Why, heavens, the Iceman cracked. She started to laugh, softly, unsteadily, giddily, and his head reared back as though a cobra had just raised its hooded head and hissed, his expression undertaking a violent transformation.

She watched it all with intense satisfaction, and laughed even harder when he snatched his arms away so abruptly that she fell flat on the floor. Adam surged to his feet and towered over her, while she rolled on to her back, stretched out her legs and leisurely crossed them at the ankles, regarding his furious black expression in merriment.

'My God, you're a lethal piece of work,' he growled from between his teeth. He looked as if he could have cheerfully murdered her and gone whistling to the hangman.

'Shot number two,' said Yvonne blandly. She laced her fingers together, put her hands behind her head and tilted it to one side, the better to read his face. 'And the first night isn't even over with. Just imagine what four-odd months of me would do to your famous composure. Bow to the inevitable, Adam. Let me go.'

He shook his head and snarled, 'Never! You're going to do the film, whether you like it or not; whether you protest or not; whether you struggle and rant and rave or not! You'll do it efficiently, on time, and with courtesy to everyone concerned, because if you don't your father won't get within a thousand miles of this project, and, as precariously as his career is balanced right now, that could mean he might never get the chance of a quality piece again! Is that clear?'

'Exceedingly,' said Yvonne succinctly in a cold voice. Her eyes were bottomless black pits of fire in a taut white face. 'I'll do your blasted little film, whether I like it or not. I'll do it with meticulous courtesy and efficiency, because I have my reputation as an excellent professional to maintain, not because you command or beg it from me. And I'll be that way for everybody concerned—but you. I'll smile, and be charming, and polite, and helpful to everyone—but you.'

'I can do without it,' he snapped contemptuously, breathing hard.

'Fair warning, then,' she said slowly.

'Fair warning.' His beautiful mouth twisted, unwillingly, it appeared, in rueful acknowledgement as he stared down at her. She cocked her pointed chin mockingly at him, and his breath escaped him in a short, unamused laugh. 'God help us both.'

He pivoted and as he strode away Yvonne murmured gently, 'Running away, my friend?'

The winter king laid a long hand along the curve of the doorknob and looked back at her. 'You and I will never be friends, Yvonne,' he said in his rich, mellifluous voice. 'That much I do guarantee you. And this I also give you for nothing: I never run away from a challenge or a fight. But your father and I have unfinished business, and I am—very much interested to see what he has to say for himself.'

He, like the maid, shut the door behind him.

Thankfully she shed the indolent supine position it had cost her so much to maintain, sat and drew her knees to her chest to huddle in a tight porcupine ball.

She dropped her face to her knees. Oh, boy, she was in at the deep end. Yet again. Tonight had been a watershed occurrence, but now what did this mean?

She scowled, and, since nobody was present to witness, it must have been for her own benefit. It meant that Adam Ruarke had a tiger by the tail; that she had to find some way to maintain her grip at the Iceman's throat. For who knew what calamitous thing might happen as they glared at each other, face to face, if one of them happened to slip?

Who knew?

Oh, she longed to be home, to be a selfish coward without pride, to care for her precious horses and look out from her front-porch step at her land, as far as the eye could see, to dream as she had dreamed these last two years away under a wide Montana sky.

She shuddered and said aloud, 'You bloody fool.'

That too must have been for her own benefit, since angels always seemed to fear treading where she went, but she doubted that she would profit from the realisation.

CHAPTER TWO

HER agent was transported into raptures.

Irritably Yvonne poured scorn on his enthusiasm. He did not appear to mind it. After she had taken his phone call, she finished dressing. The procedure took less than a minute: ancient jeans and a scarlet blouse, which Betty had ironed, and white canvas oxfords. She dragged the heavy mass of her hair to one side and braided it loosely, fastening the end with a plain rubber band and throwing the heavy length over her shoulder.

The morning after was nearly noon. The Iceman had to have moved very fast indeed, to have contacted the executive producer of the film, and the other relevant parties, then to have called her agent with a concrete offer. She hadn't even called her agent yet. Apparently the contract was already being telexed to him. It was an extraordinarily generous one; given the immense success of Adam Ruarke's films, she stood to gain a fortune from the enterprise, plus a meteoric re-entry into the industry. The point was, she'd needed neither the fortune nor the burn-up of the re-entry, but as far as blackmails went the scenario was at least an unusual one.

She wondered at Adam's role in all this. Film directors had *carte blanche* over many things, but his activity in her contract negotiations indicated that his involvement in this film was far greater than normal. Did he oversee all his films like that, or was this one special?

She ran down the stairs, long legs flashing, and went in search of her family and breakfast.

At the doorway to the dining-room, she hesitated, a vivid woman caught in mid-motion. The clan was gathered to lunch. Vivian and Christopher were laughing together over some great jest, a handsome pair of gleeful conspirators; their marriage, after thirty years, was still a huge success and one of Hollywood's celebrated anomalies.

They had visited her in Montana rarely, preferring instead to maintain contact by phone. Vivian had conceived a dislike for 'the dreaded beasts' as she called Yvonne's lovely thoroughbreds; but David, her older brother by five years, liked the ranch and was a frequent visitor in between the success of his own projects as a bitingly satirical screenwriter.

Her presence was noticed, and greeted with warmth and affection. Over a light repast of asparagus quiche and fresh fruit she caught up on all the latest sagas and gossip in her family's lives. Under the conversation she studied her father in speculation and concern. Christopher looked incredibly well for a man in his fifties, physically fit and appearing younger than his actual years, his handsome chestnut hair silvered at the temples.

Stricken anew, for some reason, by how odd it was to have a sex symbol for a father, Yvonne leaned her chin on one narrow hand and asked him, 'Did Adam and you talk last night?'

Her father regarded her with wary love. 'Yes, we did.'

The entire room had hesitated. Vivian stared with fascination at her lunch, and David studied his own hands.

A fool she might possibly be, but she wasn't stupid. Yvonne's massive eyes narrowed. She smelled a rat.

'And is everything all right?' she asked in a dangerous soft voice. If it wasn't, if the Iceman had somehow reneged on his part of the unholy bargain, she would rip him apart with her bare hands.

A heated fantasy: herself in wild fury, the winter king tall as an ivory tower crowned with flame, her hands tearing the clothes from his graceful body, his head tilted back in supplication. Yvonne shook with the beauty of it and was consumed by desire.

But her father's eyes positively sparkled with delight. 'Everything has worked out—far better than anyone could have hoped,' replied Christopher with care. 'Adam and I reached a very satisfactory agreement.'

Damn it, she felt equal measures of disappointment and relief. Was there ever such a contrary creature as herself? For her father's sake Yvonne forced a smile to her lips, and said simply, 'I'm glad.'

'And what a rare gift it is. I get the privilege of working with one of today's greatest talents, who happens also to be my very beautiful daughter,' said her father gently, and he reached for her hand to carry it to his lips. 'I love you very much, Yvonne. Thank you for what you're doing for me. We couldn't be more proud of you.'

'Oh, rubbish,' she grumbled ungraciously, for she was an inheritor of many aspects from her parents, but gentleness had not been one of them. Still, her fingers curled against her father's cheek, a fleeting, furtive caress that was nevertheless well noted by everyone in the room.

Even the new arrival.

'How touching,' lightly remarked Adam Ruarke from the doorway. Everyone stirred in surprise; the intimate relaxed atmosphere fled in violent disarray; instantly Yvonne plummeted into savagery, her face taut and feral as a wildcat as she glared at the intruder.

Who did he think he was, to stand there with the erect and regal pose of a monarch? His auburn hair was brushed sleekly from a finely defined forehead, his skin the light transparent gold of morning, that elegant mouth holding a faint, cryptic smile, his icy, beautiful eyes regarding her in wry contemplation.

His clothing was as simple and as classic as it had been the night before. The cream shirt was open at the neck, the deerskin-coloured trousers moulded to the lean grace of his hips and thighs. His body was classically proportioned, muscled and taut and clearly powerful without an ounce of excess flesh anywhere on him.

'Vivian, Christopher. Hello, David,' said Adam without taking his eyes away from her. They greeted him with easy affection. It infuriated her even further, despite the hard common sense that underlaid it: why antagonise the victorious conqueror into retribution? 'Good afternoon, Yvonne. May I say that you're looking remarkably in character today?'

Her dusky gaze shot sparks at him, and she snarled maliciously, the first ridiculous thing that came to mind, 'Your lack of freckles is an affront to nature.'

The winter king's eyes grew very wide. Unseen and unnoticed by Yvonne, her famous and dignified mother had creased up. Serene and unscathed, Adam said to her, 'You and I need to talk.'

'Privacy,' commented Christopher wisely, and her loving, traitorous family scattered like so many autumn blown leaves.

Yvonne cursed them absent-mindedly, as she lounged back in her chair in an attitude of indolence; then her hooded gaze fell on to the half-eaten meal that lay in front of her, and she shoved it away in an abrupt movement that clattered the rare, delicate china into musical discord.

'So, talk,' she growled surlily, watching out of the corner of her eye as he traversed the spacious room with meticulous ease.

'What nice weather we're having, but do you think it will ever rain?' He spoke the inanity with sardonic pointedness, as he rounded the long table and laid a package down on it.

Her fingers sought purchase, found it on something and gripped, white-knuckled. Adam laid a gentle hand over her wrist, the warm contact shaking through her senses, and he said, 'For God's sake, not the Sèvres. I'm not worth it.'

She looked down at their hands. Her own, while femininely shaped, were strong enough to hold a spirited horse in check. Adam's hands appeared slender until laid over hers, for the comparison clearly showed the male strength in the corded sinews and the expanse of the palm. The immaculately pared fingernails were half the width of hers again, and the tracery of veins along the back of his hand was a web of fine subtlety.

'No,' she agreed hoarsely, as she loosened her death-clench on her dinner plate and pulled away from him, 'you're not. What do you want?'

Even as she thrust out of her chair to prowl the open expanse of the room restlessly, she glanced back at him sidelong, and nearly checked herself. He appeared to be recovering from some impulse that had been almost overpowering; she wondered if he had longed to do her violence. Certainly she had never wished to do or dreamed of doing to another person the excessive things he drove her to. What a queer and lucid bond they had forged together!

As if in conscious contrast to her, he had gathered his body into that frigid, motionless repose he executed so incomparably, leaning against the dining-table as his vivid gaze retreated inwards in introspection. He shut himself off from her, so completely that no human or supernatural means could recall him back to this world from that private realm unless he wished it. The winter king's reign was a vast one; it was over himself.

'I brought you a script,' Adam replied. An idle hand flicked towards the package beside him, then returned to its frozen home against a hard thigh. 'First reading is Monday afternoon. Your father has the details.'

Her fast breathing was shallow and uneven. She found him insupportable. She darted forward, talons outstretched, swift as a falcon screaming out of the blue, snatched the package and threw it into the marble fireplace.

Adam exploded out of his stillness in one great uncontainable leap before he could stop himself. The leap was towards the hearth, which was empty and cold, where the package lay undamaged. He stopped dead and rounded on her, and she covered her luscious mouth with both hands in a parody of terror while her eyes danced in wicked joy.

'Poor baby,' he murmured then, in furious, tender solicitation, as he took a threatening step towards her. 'For once in your life you're not going to get your own way. What can I possibly be thinking?'

She ground her teeth, then lowered her hands and spat at him, 'I suspect that thinking is not your strongest point.'

'Certainly not around you.' His agreement was grim as his chest rose and fell visibly. He rested his hands on his lean hips, a picture of disgust. His wine hair had escaped from its original sleek containment and fell intoxicatingly over his lowering brow. 'Your destructiveness is infallible; you can level a man's logical rationality to the ground without even thinking about it, and then grind your heel into him.'

'Change your mind,' she urged him softly.

He shook his head and smiled, the swordsman blade-sharp. 'Never.'

She made a strangled sound; no doubt it would have been pithy and multisyllabic had it managed to find its way out of her throat. His grey eyes were luminous with laughter. She sprang for the fireplace, one claw-swipe capturing a box of matches, and she'd struck one alight when thunder fell upon her.

This time his hands on both her wrists were not gentle at all. The thunder bellowed out from him on the lightest, silent puff, and the flare of the match between her thumb and forefinger disappeared in a tiny sulphurous curl.

Her other hand still clutched the box. He turned her fully towards him and shook it, his handsome face taut and dark with rage. 'Drop it,' he growled from between beautiful hard teeth. She said nothing, did nothing, and he shook her harder. 'Damn you, drop it!'

She was a frozen statue. His hold tightened, powerfully, inescapably; he didn't appear even to realise what he was doing, as the slow-building pain arced her slender body and stole away her strength.

Her immense, dark, unblinking eyes were fixed on him in shock and wonder. She had never seen anything so feral, so beautiful before. She was sinking to the floor and he bowed over her, his own compulsive ravening gaze taking her apart and putting her together again, willy-nilly, and she didn't recognise herself in the new puzzle he had made of her.

Whatever he saw in her face altered his own expression. He eased to the floor, hands gentled and sliding up her forearms in a searing caress, and he said with wise and ruthless seductiveness, '*Won't* you drop it, Yvonne? Won't you drop it, *please*?'

What—what was he doing? The tiger in her was bewildered, as he let go of her arms entirely and cupped the delicate line of her jaw with probing, splayed fingers. Her confused eyes blinked, and he brought his elegant mouth down on to hers.

If last night he had been warm, now he was heated. Her breath came in on an intake of amazement, and her perfect lips parted, and he entered her mouth with unhurried, ineffable consummation, and she was ravished to the core.

She knew what a man's mouth was. She knew what it was, to be inside a man's mouth. She thought she knew the feelings that it provoked in her, the dance of tongues, the casual repartee of pleasurable movement.

She knew nothing. She was a new-born to the experience; his slow, unrelenting probe into her dark, moist crevice was a stunning execution of her former precepts; he snatched her whirling into blatant, terrifying, soul-shattering intensity. The insubstantial shades of those other times and kisses fell sacrificially under the executioner's axe, and the moan she gave up to him was an offering of sweet frankincense and bitter myrrh.

She held on to his shoulders. Well, there was nothing else to hold on to. He did not seem to be breathing, but instead was a taut victim to some terrible, devouring suspense.

She was driven, always driven; this time it was starvation that impelled her to enter him as he did her, enter that private, male, beautiful domain of sensuality, and he shook with feverish reaction as she fitted her hand to the back of his neck and plunged as hard and as deeply into him as she possibly could.

His response was molten. He made some sound, a deep, male, evocative growl of discovery in his chest, and realisation of what she was doing exploded in her head.

My God, she thought, hazed with astonishment, I am a madwoman! Making love to the enemy. Yes, that was what it was: an oral representation of the deepest sexual act.

Instantly she changed into a raging virago. She struggled, fused to his mouth and his body by the bond of his ruthless arms, and when he would not let her go she bit him. On the lip, hard.

He reared away with a gasp, and his face was a stranger's: tight and excited, with the grey eyes glittering hotly, and a slight crimson smear on his lower lip. His expression was so electrifying, the sight of him rousing a powerful, atavistic reaction in the deepest corners of her soul. Then he razed over her ferocious, terrified face and bee-stung swollen mouth with blazing silvershot eyes and dived with savage, erotic accuracy to bite her back.

He was the one to laugh, a murmurous, satisfied, intimate laugh as she fell back from him in boneless shock. This time he let her go. Her arms crossed over her chest in a classic position of defence and she sat back on her heels.

She would have shrieked at him in wordless fury had he given her the opportunity. Instead Adam's lit, translucent eyes fell to her hands and he scowled, and she realised why he had even kissed her to begin with: the devious motives of the man, the reason behind his softened approach and extraordinary sensual assault. She could not be any angrier; it just simply wasn't possible. But she could wonder, in a tiny corner of her mind, why she felt such a deadening sense of disappointment.

Ever one to snatch victory in the face of defeat, she raised the box of matches she had never relinquished, and rattled it under his patrician nose. It was crushed out of its shape; she had never even consciously retained her hold and could just as easily have let the box slide from her stunned fingers, but she would die before she admitted it to him.

Adam smiled then, sunnily, and said, as if the knowledge of it was a delight, 'You never give up, do you? You just don't know how.'

One corner of her ravished mouth lifted in a sneer. 'I certainly know of no good reason why.'

'Grace?' he suggested drily, sliding one hand under her elbow. 'Dignity? Good sportsmanship?'

'I've tried them,' replied Yvonne as drily as she allowed him to assist her to her feet. 'They seem to apply to other scenes and other people. Not to you. I've never been blackmailed or coerced in my life, and I find it a galling and infuriating spur.'

'Oh, is that what it is?' purred the Iceman, and she threw him an impatient glance. She had no time for cryptic remarks, and he, apparently, did not see fit to explain himself to her. But then she doubted if he ever bothered to explain himself to anyone. That one characteristic, at least, they appeared to have in common. 'I find myself relieved that you don't behave this way with just any man you happen to meet.'

'Who's to say,' she replied with a silken, sour smile, 'that I don't?'

He studied her in amusement and just shook his auburn head, then bent to retrieve the package from the fireplace before she could further endanger it. She shrugged, and tossed the mangled box of matches on to the mantel, and he placed the script into her hands and told her, 'Burn it, and you'll just have to acquire another copy. Don't waste your energy on useless statements.'

'No, indeed,' she agreed, slanting him a narrowed sidelong glance, 'it's time for a change of tactics anyway.'

'Unforgiving, stubborn, contrary, rude, exasperating, inventive. Relentless as well; I do believe I'm looking forward to the next trick,' he said lightly, flicking her stiff cheek with a careless finger. 'My, how you do worry at that leash.'

'Confinement,' she enunciated, her nostrils pinched, 'has never been a particular favourite of mine.'

'But no one confines you,' said the winter king unforgivably, his beautiful eyes wide, his empty, upturned hands in a graceful display. 'No contract has been signed. Walk away, my dear. Turn your back and walk away.'

He held the door open, and she stood at the threshold, but she trembled and could not take the irrevocable step. 'I can't.'

'No, because you are loyal as well.' He said it with such remarkable gentleness that she had to avert her face. 'I had a special reason for coming today, you know.'

'Oh?' she replied with a show of indifference.

'Yes.' He paused, a delicate regrouping. 'During the course of my conversation with your father last night, he explained a great many things, among them being the severe exhaustion you suffered the last year before you quit acting. Is that why you're so resistant to returning to work?'

She had gone completely quiet as he spoke, a tense, listening stillness. After searching swiftly through the rich, complex nuances of his voice for any kind of goad or taunt and finding nothing but a simple request for understanding, she replied cautiously, 'In part.'

Her face was still averted. She did not see him shift in subtle silence in order to see her expression. The striking angular bones were tight with anticipated pain, the great eloquent eyes downcast.

He was a genius at finding just the right entry-point for the verbal rapier, and could insert it so exquisitely between the tough armour plates that his victim quite often never felt pain. He said in classic simplicity, 'Yvonne, this needn't be an ordeal. I will challenge you. I can't help it. But I won't push you beyond your limits.'

For a rarity, the clever man before her knew failure, as her proud, unique face twisted into an agony that would return to haunt him. 'You won't have to,' she said with a bitterness that was unanswerable. 'For, you see, I'm all too capable of doing that myself.'

She found that Adam's judgement was infallible. The screenplay was nothing short of brilliant. She knew without doubt that the movie would be the finest thing she had ever participated in, and had the potential, under the auspices of a deft and wise directorship, to become regarded as a classic for years to come. She wondered, with final calm, if she was facing her own destruction.

The next few days and events moved to an inexorable whirlwind machine. Contracts were signed, returned, timetables set, information was given on the preparations made for the cast and crew to be maintained on location in Arizona, both Yvonne's and Christopher's measurements were taken by the costume designer, publicity options were discussed.

She did lunch, Hollywood-style, with old acquaintances who professed delight and avid curiosity at her reappearance, and exchanged witticisms over salad and Perrier while divulging nothing about herself, and she lay alone in the dark, sleepless hours before dawn in endless, compulsive speculation.

Adam telephoned her on Sunday afternoon. She'd known other directors to be at a screaming point at the unbelievable pressure of staying on schedule and within a budget and still achieving a quality product. Adam's reputation had some basis, for he sounded as serene as the eye of a hurricane. Iceman, ship's captain, god.

Betty answered the phone, and when she took it in her bedroom he said without preamble, 'Yvonne, the Press are going wild.'

'Indeed?' she murmured, lying back on her bed, ankles crossed. She was exhausted.

'They're screaming to get you into a conference. Movie star disappears off the face of the earth for two years and makes a triumphant return, that sort of thing. I've never seen anything quite like it,' he said.

Her smile was involuntary. He did sound surprised, in a sleepy kind of way. 'They like me,' Yvonne said. 'I've always maintained a good relationship with the Press.'

'They're a pack of wolves that'll fawn all over you or tear you apart at a moment's notice,' he said in wry, pithy reply. 'I can see how you would understand each other.'

She laughed out loud, wondering if he had seen any of the gossip columns recently. A prominent columnist had been present at her parents' party, and she and the Iceman had figured over-largely—even luridly—in the recounting of it. 'Your mistake. I never fawn.'

'Well, if we don't throw them some titbits, this time they might go for blood. Are you possibly up for a conference? We could make it a short one.'

So he was acting as publicity agent as well? Just how much control did he have over this film?

Her smile widened. 'Why not?'

'Are you sure?' He sounded cautious. 'I know it's a damned nuisance, but PR's shouting the sooner the better. If it's convenient, perhaps after the reading tomorrow...'

'Don't worry,' said Yvonne gently, which was always when she was at her most dangerous. 'I can handle it.'

The next day she and Christopher travelled together to the studio for the first reading, and they met the rest of the cast, which was unusually small. The focus of the script was unrelentingly simplistic and drew upon the complexities of just a few relationships.

Each of the other three present had achieved a noteworthy reputation. Yvonne was impressed but did not show it; she entered in a silent, sultry stalk behind her elegant father, dressed as carelessly as ever, in ragged chinos and a faded black T-shirt and scuffed Adidas tennis shoes, gleaming chestnut hair in a riotous tangle, her clear and perfect complexion not even powdered.

One other man, dark-haired and ruggedly handsome, and two women. The two other women present were formidably arrayed, in sophisticated suits that screamed *haute couture*, striking and beautiful and immaculate from their painted nails to the three layers of mascara on their long lashes. Such relentless self-marketing. They both eyed Yvonne's appearance in considerable startlement and some distaste; she just blinked at them and smiled sleepily, and claimed a comfortable, leather-padded chair at one end of the chrome and walnut boardroom.

Five minutes to go. She hooked another chair around to face her and put her feet up. Her father lay waste to the room with his indubitable charm. The actresses were enchanted. So was Yvonne.

The door to the room opened and settled. The winter king had arrived.

He was timeless, in black trousers and long-sleeved black turtleneck, the lovely clothes hugging that lean male body to devastating effect. The breadth of his muscled chest and shoulders, the accordion slimness of his waist and tight hips, the flare of long, defined thighs were shadowed and sinuously fluent. The high neck emphasised the sheer precision of his handsome face, and the brilliance of those beautiful eyes. The colour of his auburn hair gleamed with immeasurable depth; the gold tan of his skin and his elegant mouth paled to the colour of antique ivory.

The room hushed. It was an outstanding accolade. Yvonne's breath had caught in her throat at the stunning sight of him; she refused to acknowledge it.

A smile of pure amusement creased Adam's face as he caught sight of her. It was banished in the next instant by a stern, sharp frown as he took in the empty expanse of the table in front of her. Everyone else had their script with them and open at the beginning scene.

Her massive dark eyes watched him with the bland speculation of a scientist inspecting an insect as he strode over to her and slapped his copy of the screenplay in front of her. Her blank gaze fell to it, and rose to his icy, tight-lipped stare. Menace went before the winter king like a black-cloaked herald. It touched her with chill psychic fingers, and warned. She did not move from her indolent pose.

He turned, smiled upon the others with seductive charm, and performed introductions between the actors and a wonderfully executed, concise dissertation on his intended goals.

Where before her father had sought to impress and succeeded, Adam's charismatic presence reigned in effortless supremacy. Neither Christopher nor the other male actor appeared to mind the advent of such an ascendant personality in the least. They were clearly expanding in warm enjoyment under the other man's sorcerous spell.

The two actresses drooled. Yvonne watched them in clinical fascination. She wanted to rake her nails across their gorgeous faces, yank their moussed and hennaed hair out by the roots. Her graceful sleek eyebrows quirked in surprise at her own savage whimsy.

'Yvonne,' said Adam with terrible, threatening gentleness, 'pay attention.'

She jerked in startlement and said, 'Three bags full, sir.'

Everyone else in the room laughed. Even the actresses did, in warm surprise. Well, she had said it with such winsome, lethal charm, hadn't she?

Adam looked neither charmed nor reproving. 'We're about to start the reading,' he said. His patience was an insult.

She gave it back to him, a dark and satanic mirror. 'I am aware of that.'

His frigid, fierce eyes were pitiless. He was even more gentle. 'You have the opening lines.'

She was warm with gratitude. 'An honour, in such a beautifully crafted script.'

His elegant mouth was granite, speared with sticks of precision dynamite about to blow. 'Don't you think you had better open your copy?'

Yvonne held the winter king's hawkish gaze without moving. Her smile was creamy. She gave him her opening lines flawlessly. He sat frozen. The others were quick to contribute theirs, and the reading lasted for well over an hour and a half. The screenplay he had placed before her remained untouched the entire time.

Finally Adam stopped the reading and told everyone in the room, and his ironic glance did not flick towards her once, 'Thank you for a remarkable first performance.'

He conducted a question-and-answer session, addressed them individually, and concluded the meeting. What a pinnacle of self-control he was, and how she looked forward to bringing him down from it.

Under the general relaxation and dispersement, he prowled over to retrieve his script and paused to consider her. 'Your memory is photographic?'

His sardonic comment was exactly what he had asked for, and no more than she deserved, and yet it stung. 'No,' she replied, 'my memory is compulsive and perfectionist.'

He checked whatever it was he had been about to say, and looked at her sharply. 'I thought you did it to goad me.'

'I certainly goaded you with it,' she agreed.

'Why do you do it to yourself?' he asked in a quiet voice, his eyes hard.

Her lips wanted to tremble, but she held them tight. She had baited him, and he had used intimidation tactics on her, and they had circled and sparred with each other for over two hours, but only now, at the end, was he finally, truly angry. For the life of her she couldn't figure out why.

'I'm hungry and thirsty and I have a Press conference to face as soon as I walk out that door,' she said, carefully retreating from the inexplicable. 'Leave me alone, Adam.'

He glared at her, his face darkened with thunder-clouds, then he pivoted to stalk out of the room. Yvonne sighed and dug the heels of her hands into her tired eyes.

There was a tentative touch on her shoulder. She obliged it by looking over her hands enquiringly. The younger actress, Sally, smiled at her. 'I just wanted to let you know what a pleasure it is to meet you,' said the other woman. 'Your work has so impressed me.'

Good God, the other woman actually meant it. She was looking sincerity in the face. Yvonne's soul knew a dark and self-directed violence. She searched for kindness, discovered tattered remnants, and gifted Sally with a sweetness in her returning smile that the other actress treasured. Give it away, give it all away. She didn't know what else to do with it.

'Thank you,' she said warmly. 'I look forward to working with you. By the end of this, we should all be good friends, don't you think?'

You and I will never be friends, Yvonne...

She rose, stiff as an old woman from sitting so long, and went out to converse with the PR secretary waiting in the nearby office, who led her to the dozen or so waiting journalists. It was a very small, controlled conference. How cleverly titillating. She recognised Adam behind the idea.

There was a table and chair, and hot lights. Yvonne took the chair, a ragged-clothed queen on a throne. She greeted the journalists she remembered by name, and they fell in love with her again, and cameras flashed and a babble of questions roared at her.

She held up a narrow hand, and grinned her pleasure at them as they gave her silence. 'We shall play a game,' she said, her dark eyes dancing. 'You get to ask me anything you like, but I only answer yes or no. Let's see how inventive you can be with that.'

The ones who knew her gave a theatrical groan. They knew her games. She would tease and tantalise them, flirt unblushingly, be generous with praise and certain information, and sit blank as a stone at viciousness or impertinence gone too far. All in all, it was good Press. They were all professionals doing their jobs.

The questions started. She was silent with the ones she couldn't answer with a yes or no; and so she kept secret her private life in Montana, and they could not claim offence. They actually acquired quite a lot of information, and began to vie with each other as to the cleverness of their questions.

She waited. Sure enough, what she waited for came.

'Ms Trent, is it true that you walked up to a total stranger and slapped him at your parents' party?' shouted one intrepid genius.

Thank you, she told him silently, as she beamed and said, 'Yes.'

'Was it all a misunderstanding, just as your agent said?'

'No.'

They were gobbling it up. 'Is it true that your victim was Adam "the Iceman" Ruarke, who's now executive producer and director of your new film?'

My new film? She smiled. 'Yes.'

'And what did he do when you slapped him?' a re-markably stupid one asked, but they had to try. She laughed merrily. They were practically foaming at the mouth.

A graceful black movement from behind the pack of journalists caught her eye. Yvonne's eyes narrowed against the glare of the hot lights. The winter king settled against the back wall, a silent snowfall at midnight.

'Are you getting along together now?' another shouted. How incredibly blind they all were. All their attention was on her spitfire and shadows.

Adam's sexy mouth smiled at her.

She dug into her ragged chinos, produced a quarter, flipped the coin and caught it in one deft fist. They were guffawing by the time she'd slapped it on to the table and peered under her hand dubiously. Then her eye-brows shot to her hairline. She said in amazement, 'Yes?'

The answer brought the house down.

CHAPTER THREE

ADAM was not at all angered by her little performance. In fact, he laughed as hard as the rest of them.

Disgruntlement glittered briefly in her eyes and was at once banished to the nethermost corners of her mind. Thankfully the slip of her façade had come during a time when the cameras had been quiet; she knew better than anyone how dangerous it was to be unguarded in front of people who watched, shark-like, for any slip at all.

The conference was concluded in short, climactic order as Adam pushed away from the wall and slowly traversed the edge of the room. One by one the journalists fell silent as they became aware of his cat-like presence. Yvonne watched him with immense respect. His lean male face was serene and unclouded, that black-clad, muscular body fluid with masterful choreography, his elegant mouth inscrutable.

He ignored the shouted questions and strolled up to Yvonne. The air was blinding with white explosions. Her head fell back to look at him. His smiling, icy grey eyes were deadly with purpose. A warning detonated, too late, inside her head.

Adam laid an inexorable hand on her arm and said gently, 'Time to go, darling.'

Her sculpted lips parted. He gave her no time to say it, but braced his powerful legs and heaved. She was launched into the air and landed with appalling, breathtaking force on the rock-hard pillar of his shoulder. She whoofed as her stomach made contact, her long, magnificent mane of hair floating riotously about her head. He wrapped an arm around her long legs, fireman-style, while her astonished gaze blinked at the debilitating sight of his lean, flat buttocks and long flanks. The tip of her hair brushed the backs of his knees.

The place was in an uproar. She heard the cacophony dimly through the roar in her own ears. By the time she had recovered enough to shriek, 'What's this?' Adam had exited the room and was walking down the hall in long, easy strides.

'Good Press?' he murmured. The growl of his voice rumbled through her stomach and thighs and utterly destroyed any sense of composure she might have hoped to achieve.

Her head bobbed with every step he took. She swiped her hair to one side with a wobbling hand, and craned her neck to look at the débâcle Adam had left behind them.

She was in time to catch the sight of two photographers attempting to lunge through the doorway at the same time. They stuck, and glared at each other, struggling, until one shot through with such force, he lost his balance and went down like a ton of bricks. Then the other staggered, attempted to climb over the first one, and fell on top of him. Adam had paused at the end of the hall to punch the lift button. By the time the doors opened, the two photographers down the hall had come to blows, and Yvonne was laughing like a hyena.

The lift doors closed. Adam asked, 'Did they catch it?'

'No,' she said, strangled on her own mirth.

'A pity,' he grunted, then, 'Stop struggling, damn it.'
She struggled all the harder. 'Put me down!'

'No.' She pinched his thigh, hard. The lift doors
opened as he slapped her on the derrière. Hard. She
yelped like a whipped puppy.

He strode with her through the ground floor of the
studio offices. She felt as though the pressure in her face
would make her explode, and shouted at him, 'Where
are you taking me?'

'To dinner.' Adam nodded calmly at the two suited
executives and uniformed guard in the lobby who had
turned to gape at them, and he paused to hitch the wrig-
gling woman higher on to his shoulder.

'How dare you? My father's waiting to take me home!'
she yelled, in the hope that their witnesses would decide
to take action against the crime being committed. The
two executives hurried out of the lobby in opposite di-
rections while the startled guard backed into a potted
plant.

'My God, you're a noisy woman. I sent him home,'
replied the Iceman, who tightened his iron grip on her
kicking legs. 'Yvonne,' he said then, reasonably, 'if you
don't stop this, I shall very likely drop you on your head.'

'You can't afford to!' she snapped, then crossed her
arms and propped herself against the small of his
sinuous, rippling back. 'The lawsuit would cripple you.'

He laughed and strode out of the doors into the glaring
heat of Southern California's autumnal sun. She said,
'Adam?'

There was the slightest wary hesitation in his voice.
'Yes?'

'My head's pounding and my face hurts.'

He stopped on the pavement. 'If I put you down will you promise to come to dinner with me and behave like a good girl?'

Behave like a good girl? A—good...girl? She gritted her teeth. By the time they finished the damned film, she would very likely need dentures. But he was waiting for her reply, so she said humbly, 'Yes, Adam.'

For every clever man there had to be the occasional moment of foolishness. He set her on her feet gently, and the relief to her escalated blood-pressure was inexpressible as she came upright, her wild hair a concealing chestnut cloud about her head and shoulders.

Like a starving man invited to the king's banquet he sank his hands into the glorious untamed mass and brushed it back from her burning red face. He got just one glance of her whitened lips and dark eyes snapping with furious hilarity.

Then she was bounding away from him, a loosed and graceful falcon intoxicated with flight. Her long legs flashed in the sun in distance-preying strides, her exquisite throat exposed as she turned her face to the sky and laughed. The man she left behind could no more refuse to chase her than he could give up breathing, and he followed her along an erratic, heedless path finally to pin her between two parked limousines.

It was her hair, again, her pride and downfall. He gained on her enough to sink a great fist into it, and she was hauled to a precipitate stop with a ungentle yank that made her squawk like a stuck bird.

He pulled her back against his chest. She was heated and trembling with a bizarre exhilaration, and the man who had carried her not inconsiderable weight with such effortless strength throughout an entire large building was breathing heavily, his heartbeat slamming into her shoulderblades with machine-gun speed.

He put a long arm around her shoulders. She rested her chin on it and stared broodingly at the rear tyre of one limousine. When he buried his face into the side of her palpitating neck, she wanted to melt all over the pavement. 'Yvonne?' whispered Adam, moving his lips on her salted skin.

'What?' she sighed, her heavy eyelids drooping.

'I'm hungry and thirsty too. Will you please have dinner with me?' The quivering tension in her slender body eased, and she leaned against the greater length of him, the falcon come to perch at last.

'All right,' she murmured, hardly aware of what she agreed to.

He shook against her. She thought it was laughter. 'All it took was a please?' he said, muffled against her flesh. 'Then why didn't that work last week when you nearly burnt your script?'

She was not aware that she leaned shudderingly into the caress of his mouth. 'I don't know. Sometimes it works and sometimes it doesn't.'

He turned her around, anchored his arm on her shoulders and matched his longer stride to hers as they walked back through the car park. She glanced at him sidelong and found to her bewilderment that his handsome face was as untroubled and serene as ever. He caught her glance and asked her, 'Have you always been so contrary?'

Her frown was fierce. 'As long as I can remember,' she said with resignation.

'I can remember the time I saw your first photograph,' he said, his grey eyes sparkling. 'You were an enchanting sight, elfin and tiny and snuggled against your mother's breast, your dark eyes peering at the camera in such wide, unaffected surprise.'

Her untidy head turned on him fully in an exact replica of that old amazement. She said incredulously, 'You were a subscriber to *Vogue* magazine at—what, age thirteen, fourteen?'

His beautiful mouth twitched. They had halted at a steel-grey BMW convertible, and he fished his keys out of a pocket to unlock the doors. 'I was fourteen, and not exactly a subscriber,' said Adam in self-directed mockery. 'But I did buy that one copy. I was—in the throes of my first love, you see. And if you tell Vivian that, I shall strangle you.'

Yvonne found herself grinning in huge enjoyment as she slid bonelessly into her seat. Heavens, how did she come to be so relaxed with the enemy? He was a sly one, to be sure, but what would it hurt to call a truce for the space of one quick meal? What harm could one insignificant dinner possibly have?

He slid into the driver's seat, started the car and pulled out of his reserved space. She combed her narrow fingers through her tangled hair, struggling to bring it to some semblance of order, and as she worried at one particularly stubborn knot she told him, 'You should know better than to give me more ammunition.'

The winter king remarked unperturbably, 'Young lady, you don't need ammunition. Your bare hands are sufficient weapons on their own.'

The car slid to a stop at the security gate, he waved at the guard who nodded and raised the gate, and the BMW shot through. She glared at her lean, relaxed companion and grumbled something under her breath about sharpened ice-picks. Adam sent her a brief glance, and his expression undertook a swift transformation, and he laughed aloud.

She scowled even harder, and snapped, 'What?'

'Look at you,' he said deeply, his grey eyes brilliant. 'Sitting there, scowling your bad temper, muttering evil spells and weaving them with sunshine through your hair. You're a witch-woman, and a menace to civilised society.'

'I like that!' she breathed, highly offended. 'An agreement to one simple dinner, and he takes it as an invitation to throw insults—stop the car, damn it. I've changed my mind.'

'Tough luck.' He slammed the accelerator to the floor and the BMW roared powerfully as it hit the open highway. 'You've already agreed, and I'm going to hold you to it. You no longer have a choice in the matter.'

'I hardly had a choice to begin with,' she snapped, her dark eyes throwing hot sparks. She was intent on working herself into a fine fury, and succeeding wonderfully.

'No, I know,' he replied coolly as he frowned at the expanse of the road in front of him. Suddenly, though their physical proximity could be measured in bare inches, he felt very far away. She was disconcerted and troubled, and hid her perplexing reactions under her speculative stare. 'You're forever rebelling against any authority or show of decisive strength. It's an instinctive, knee-jerk reaction for you, isn't it? Is that also part of the reason you finally broke away from the career your parents had guided you into?'

'What?' she burst out, considerably startled, and then she smiled and shook her head. 'Oh, heavens, you do have the wrong end of the stick, don't you? No, my parents were everything wise and loving and supportive. I admire them tremendously. Even as a six-year-old child I was a headstrong horror, and I'd enjoyed the photo sessions with my mother so much that I demanded to be allowed to do it again.'

'And they obliged?' he asked, a careless prompt. He hardly appeared to be paying attention, so remote did he seem, a lounging figure in the archetypical colours of crimson, and white and black; he looked as though he belonged in some ancient fable, and talking to him was as easy as talking to herself.

'They were delighted,' she replied. 'School wasn't enough to keep me challenged, and I had gone through three nannies already. So they contracted an agent, and proceeded to let me have my head. Within reason, that is. They did keep a stern check on the number of bookings I was allowed to do. I was given everything I could possibly want.'

'So what happened?' Adam asked, spearing her with lucid grey.

Yvonne's expression was a self-inflicted irony. 'Nothing happened,' she said drily. 'I happened. Everything that has occurred in my life, anything that has gone wrong, has come from me. It's funny, but your parents can give you everything in the world, but they can't teach you what to do with it. That, you have to learn for yourself.'

He shook his rich auburn head. 'I don't believe you.'

Her eyebrows rose in startlement. 'About my parents?'

'About everything that went wrong in your life happening because you caused it,' he replied quietly. 'I've heard some horror stories about the last year you worked, from other professionals who'd been involved in the productions. From the sound of it you could neither assume responsibility for what happened nor control it.'

Yvonne went into a shut-down sequence. She felt as if he had reached into her chest and squeezed her heart, and it hurt, dreadfully. Just his quiet words could evoke the memory of the trap that last year had been for her, of contractual obligations, commitments made, demands, so many demands; she'd been drowning in the sea of demands while everything around her went to hell.

Her angular face was dead white, dark eyes like stone. 'No?' She said the word as a challenge. 'Maybe not, but it was up to me to deal with it.'

He parked the car and sat frozen. Impelled into the memory of that awful, anguished year, she stared into space and never noticed her surroundings. 'And you feel somehow that you didn't,' remarked Adam, a quiet prompting as he looked at his hands clenched on the steering-wheel. 'But I've seen those films, Yvonne. The quality of your work was completely consistent. Where's the failure in that?'

'Well. There's a question,' she replied in an absent tone, compulsively twisting her fingers around a long strand of hair she'd just unknotted, over and over and over. 'I suppose it started in little ways. I'd forget what I was talking about in the middle of a cast party. I'd drive down the street on automatic pilot, and when I would "wake up" I wouldn't remember where I was supposed to go or what I was doing. I'd be in the middle of shooting a scene and feel this hot panic wash over me because I'd blank out, or I'd be afraid that the lines I remembered belonged to another movie. The last time—the worst time—was when I woke up and couldn't remember what country I was in, or what my name was.'

The man beside her remembered to breathe, and it was a scraping, pleasureless experience. 'I think I can guess the rest,' he said harshly. 'It ended; you would have had to end it, in order to save yourself. Somehow you lost sight of Yvonne in the face of all those other personalities everyone expected from you.'

'Yes,' she said with ungovernable viciousness. 'Yes, and yes, and yes. Now, if your curiosity is satisfied, I've had more than enough of this topic of conversation. I don't want to talk about it again!'

'Then we won't,' said Adam gently, and his gentleness was the final, terrible straw.

She unbuckled her seatbelt, scrambled out of the car, and ran heedlessly down a long flight of steps, then paused in a surprise that was great enough to shake her out of her dark mood.

She looked around her. They were at the beach? What?

She was standing in the middle of a wooden stairway that led down to the Pacific, and the sparkling ocean and wide expanse of the bowl blue sky were panoramic. She took great breaths of the salt-fresh air, and the floating gulls overhead screamed their raucous cry, and a fierce, eager smile lightened her intense expression. Freedom, freedom; it was all around and within her, and she flew down the rest of the stairs, giddy and drunken with the immensity of it.

She barely halted in her headlong dash to tear off her shoes, and roll her trousers to her knees. Then she didn't stop until she stood at the edge of forever and watched it curl foaming at her narrow feet.

She was alone for a while. She retreated at last above the tidemark and sat on the dry sand, dreamily watching the incandescent reflection of the westward sun on the water. On her face was the first real peace she had known since returning to LA, when Adam came to sit beside her.

She murmured accusingly without looking at him, 'You promised me dinner.'

'You changed your mind,' he told her drily, to which she shot him a self-deprecating grin, and her eyes fell on what he held in both hands, and she laughed out loud.

He must carry spare clothing in the back of the BMW, for he had changed his black turtleneck for a crisp white T-shirt. He handed her one of the hot dogs and a soft drink he'd purchased from a waterfront vendor up on the promenade where he'd parked.

For a moment she couldn't decide which she wanted more, as she looked from the food to the drink. Then she took a huge bite of the hot dog, and balanced it on one thigh as she wiped the dirty top of the aluminum can with the edge of her shirt and opened it.

'You surprise me,' she said to him with her mouth full. 'I don't know why, but you do. I had expected something a little more along the lines of——'

'*Haute cuisine*?' he supplied with a wry smile, as words failed her and she waved an inadequate hand. 'I do like a good restaurant, but, taking my cue from your state of dress, I suspected you wouldn't be in the mood to appreciate a three-course meal with a wine list, an exclusive clientele and a supercilious *maître d'*. Of course, I could have been wrong.'

'No,' she said slowly, her dark eyes narrowed on his imperturbable face, 'you're rarely that. Clever man that you are. Why did you give up acting?'

'Because I didn't have time for both acting and directing,' he said easily, squinting against the angle of sunlight as he glanced up at the sky. It brought into relief tiny lines fanning from the corners of his dark-lashed, light-coloured eyes, laughter-lines embedded in gold. He shot her a quick glance and a twisted smile. 'I was a good actor. I'm a better director, though, and I enjoy my work.'

'You're a stunning director, and you know it,' she said deliberately as she watched him.

'Oh, but I'm modest as well,' he said, with such adroit demureness that she laughed again.

'Parents?' she queried.

'A matched pair, still intact.'

'Siblings?'

'No, but an army of cousins within a stone's throw of home just outside Edinburgh.' He finished his hot dog and settled back on the sand, propped on his elbows, his eyes mild. He didn't appear to mind her grilling.

'Why America?' she asked abruptly, sifting sand through her fingers and twirling idle circles.

He smiled. 'Why not?'

'You said Edinburgh is home,' she prodded.

He laughed at that. 'I regret my unintentional slip if you're going to behave like that. Edinburgh is where I grew up. It's where my parents live. I have a London flat, and own a condominium here in LA, but they're both just roofs over the head. Nice enough, I suppose, but I have no abiding allegiance to either place. I haven't set foot in the London flat in six months now. Where is home for you, Yvonne?'

Startled by his turn-around of the conversation, she looked at him and remained silent. His face darkened as the silence stretched into something eloquent, and then he laughed, angrily, and said in a harsh voice, 'No man's land? All right, I apologise for my intrusiveness.'

She glanced at him through her lashes, and couldn't explain the slow impulse that made her say, almost indifferently, 'No one knows. No one else beside my parents, and my brother David, and my agent. No one at all from LA or from the life I used to live here.'

Another silence, drawn into the air around them, which nearly resembled the peacefulness they had achieved at the beginning on the beach. Then he said quietly, 'If you should ever choose to share that with me, I wouldn't tell a soul. I promise you that.'

She looked at the approaching sunset and knew that he would keep that promise. 'Thank you.'

'Any—er—involvements back wherever it is that you call home?' asked Adam then, lightly. He was laughing at her, with a deft and gentle wickedness that reached inside and tugged seductively at her heartstrings.

Her lips pulled into a twisted grin of their own volition. 'Some important people,' she replied, her eyes amused. 'But no—er—involvements. And you?'

'And I?' he mocked indolently. She didn't rise to it, and he admitted, 'There've been a few.'

'One in particular in London, I seem to recall,' she mused, her eyes heavy-lidded. 'According to the gossip columns. The whatsit was rather stunning too.'

'The "whatsit" happens to be a highly successful model, with a name and a identity of her own,' he said drily.

She shrugged in lofty indifference. 'I wouldn't remember.'

He made a sound, as if smothering something. 'No, you wouldn't, would you? At any rate, the whatsit is past history.'

'So?' She dusted off her hands with great efficiency, and stated, 'I want to go home now.'

'In a minute.' She had made no move to rise to her feet, but his hand came out to shackle her wrist. She stared at it and tried to prod herself into taking offence, but she had committed too many acts of provocation against the man, and found to her weary surprise that his actions were only reasonable after all.

He continued to lounge on the sand, apparently enjoying the peace and the lingering warmth of the day, but the mood had been destroyed for her. She sat tensely, facing forward, her jaw knotted and her eyes unseeing and hard.

She would not look at him again. He should always be seen this way, bathed in the rose and gold and royal purple of sunset, a monarch reclining at ease against a tawny, seashell-embroidered carpet. No battles to fight, no armies left to conquer, a man so indelibly sure of himself and his domain that he invariably roused in everyone else an utter faith in his own capabilities. Yvonne, who fought everything, could hardly comprehend it.

He was one of the golden people, those rare and sparkling few individuals who redefined any part of the world they chose to inhabit, and if she was with him too long he would redefine her as well. He wouldn't be able to help it. He wouldn't have to do a thing. It would happen simply because he existed, and he was who he was; and, being who she was, she could not allow it.

She worried at the possible various angles of approach, then stumbled upon a possible weak link.

'Adam?' she said quietly, her eyes massive and blind.

He stirred and languidly murmured, 'Hmm?'

'If I ask you to,' she whispered, 'if I—ask—very seriously, will you cancel my contract and let me go?'

Time stretched in a measurable, uninterrupted stream that flowed between and around and through them, and became a minute, and then two.

'No,' said the winter king at last, his voice a musical chain that he hung around her lovely neck as he rose from his rest and pulled her upright along with him. She looked at him in mute grief, for he was beautiful, and hard, and inaccessible once again, and yet he could reach across that gulf and touch her; still, he could touch her.

His grey eyes held her in ruthless tenderness, and he said, 'I will not confine you. I will not try to change you. I will not check your headstrong spirit, or attempt to pour you into another mould. But I will keep you, Yvonne. I will keep you.'

'Only for now,' she warned fiercely, in a voice that shook.

He agreed with her. 'For now.'

It was such a strange observation to make, but there was a quality in that rich velvet voice that sounded like mercy: mercy, given to her, in a verbal acknowledgement of the brevity of their contract and the transience of their relationship, and it was inconceivable, unimaginable how he had managed to inflict on her the greatest hurt to date. He did it by being kind. He did it, and she could not see how or why or what he did it with.

The insignificant dinner was over with, and the harm done was incalculable.

Impetuously she threw down the terms of the truce, and took up battle once again. She goaded him, and, looking considerably surprised, he snapped back at her.

By the time he had driven her back to Beverly Hills, his elegant mouth was tight and his dark brows lowering, and she was morbidly gleeful at the destruction of their fleeting camaraderie.

He climbed out of the car when she did. Out of the corner of her eye she caught the twisting slide of his long, powerful body coming to its full height, and she whirled to snap at him, 'Don't bother seeing me to the door! You're not invited!'

His auburn head turned towards her in awesome, deliberate menace, and he snarled very quietly, 'Shut up, Yvonne. Just—shut —up.'

How far was too far with him? she wondered. Was it too far to push him too far? Was that what she wanted? Was too far just far enough?

She had hesitated, and she should have known better. He'd stalked around the end of the car and grabbed her, and she jerked away and cried out, 'You know nothing better than how to manhandle, do you?'

'You're the only woman in the world I've ever met who's asked for it!' he roared. Dear God, he was a fine one in a fury. They stalked, pace for pace and glare for glare, and a good three feet apart, to the door.

It opened before they reached it; their raised voices must have been better than a doorbell. Betty stood in the doorway, her expression determinedly bright to the man who had scared the wits out of her the week before. 'Mr Ruarke,' squeaked the maid. 'How are you today?'

'Oh, just bloody fine,' he snarled, his whole appearance an expression of danger.

The exchange was so excruciating, Yvonne's patience snapped. Before she had pretended, but now it truly did snap. 'Dear God, not *pleasantries*!' she cried.

'Woman, what else would you have me do?' he shouted.

'Oh, just go home!' Yvonne leaped inside the house, pushing the maid out of the way, and slamming the door so that the entire front of the mansion seemed to shake.

Vivian drifted out, noted the thunderous look on her daughter's face and how she pressed back against the door, her chest heaving, with her arms spread wide as if to turn aside a marauding horde, and said cheerfully, 'Yvonne's home.'

Yvonne jumped at the violent roar of the BMW, and the subsequent squeal of tyres on the driveway. 'Oh, Ms Trent,' said the trembling maid beside her. 'That one's temper is awful when he gets riled—why do you goad him so much?'

'He bothers me,' she said dreamily, and leaned her head against the door.

CHAPTER FOUR

THE first month of work on the film blew past to the dictates of a whirlwind machine.

The machine was a powerhouse of inexhaustible energy, and had a name and a face, both of which were guaranteed to interrupt a peaceful night's sleep. Adam's involvement in the film was intimate and manifold, and his personality permeated everything Yvonne witnessed.

She didn't have to see him to feel his presence in the next few weeks that followed their dinner on the beach. She could sense the brilliant, incisive mind behind the decisions that informed, directed and guided them all; in the memos that arrived for her, slashed with his hard, spiky signature; in the choice of location and the excellent planning in each updated schedule; in the anticipation of the individual's needs while maintaining a harmonious whole.

Yvonne was no businesswoman, but she was experienced. She had been involved in a few projects that had been in a scramble, and one in particular that had been a nightmare of bad planning and luck. The utter smoothness of this operation was a revelation of expertise.

She had wondered, when she'd found out that Adam was not only director but also executive producer of the film, and now she knew with instinctive depth that he would not delegate anything he could do himself, and certainly, if he did delegate, he would not simply trust that a thing would be done but would watch, quietly hawkish, for any imminent failure so that he could intervene at the earliest opportunity.

Such compulsive attention to detail on a huge project might have broken another man. It must be a punishing schedule he set for himself, an unrelenting seven-day week, but Adam appeared to thrive on the pressure. He was an awesome example of immense vitality held in effortless check for the marathon ahead of him, a racing car on cruise control, the powerful engine well oiled and purring.

She couldn't explain, even to herself, why it made her crazy to see him do everything so superbly, so effortlessly. She admired it, she really did. She was in awe of his irrefutable serenity, his indomitable patience, his incredible efficiency.

And while she was undeniably impatient and ungentle by nature, while her own powerful emotions sometimes amazed and confused her, she was not by nature destructive towards anything or anyone other than herself. Her own unrelentingly high standards were her major strength and weakness, for his assessment of her that evening by the beach was shrewdly accurate: she might make allowances and be capable of compassion for anyone else, but she did not know how to forgive herself. It was a characteristic imbued with arrogance, but Yvonne had come to accept it.

What she could not accept was how Adam prompted in her a keen violence of reaction. She burned continually to tear away his ineffable supremacy, to break that distant gulf he lay between himself and the outside world, to darken the serenity of his contained, handsome,

gold-hued features into a blood flush, and her own de-
sires appalled her.

Why she felt it she could not understand, unless it
was, perhaps, the desperate need to change him before
he changed her, to bring the winter king down to the
world of mortality, to drag him off the pedestal he
seemed to deserve so richly, to reach behind that perfect
exterior and discover a multitude of unforgivable flaws
so that she could look at him in contempt and walk away
unscathed.

No one else held her in check those first few weeks,
for no one could. She held herself in check, trembling
with the internal struggle, her great lovely eyes eloquent
with reined-in force and terror. Her conversation was
muted, the angles and hollows of her face blank and
unrevealing, the comportment of her graceful body
studied and meticulously deliberate.

The result was not colourless; quite the opposite. She
was unaware of the fact that everyone exposed to her
presence watched her in uncomprehending, amazed fascination, for she was a sultry-pitched vibration; she
hummed with magnificent unpredictability, a powder-
keg with a lit fuse of unknown length, dynamite about
to blow.

Final preparations for the location were wrapped up
while Adam guided the cast through the last of their
rehearsals and long, exhausting hours of arguing, brain-
storming, group interaction and methodology. They
bonded in mutual respect and utilisation of each other's
talents; they couldn't help but do so under Adam's wise
and unfailing direction. Yvonne found the experience
humbling and quite extraordinary.

She took advantage of the long weekend respite he gave them to fly home. She was due on location Monday morning, but for a few precious days she sought obsessively a temporary escape from the inexorable procession of events that had claimed her life. To her grief and fury, she did not find relief, for she brought the film, her character, her unquiet, terrifying emotions and the pervasive memory of Adam with her.

The ranch was fine. Her housekeeper and ranch manager, an earthy and wholly lovable husband and wife team, were fine. Her herd of fifty thoroughbred horses were fine. The stable hands were fine. They were all delighted to see her, of course, and professed to miss her and asked when she was coming home for good.

She believed their sincerity, knew they loved her, and she loved them in return down to the last foul-mouthed, good-hearted ranch hand, but the weekend was unbearably bland and untroubled. She wanted to cry or scream for the loss she felt, and instead flew to Phoenix, Arizona on Sunday afternoon with the sense of escape she had sought by returning home in the first place. She felt like a thoroughly bewildered traitor. It was not an experience to engender a good mood.

She prowled through the baggage claim area and stalked out of the departure gate, her hair ruthlessly yanked away from her taut face in a tight, confining braid, dark sunglasses hiding the restless confusion in her eyes.

Richard, her 'husband' in the film, had agreed to pick her up at the airport. It was a four-hour turn-around drive from the location and she just as easily could have taken a car from the Hertz rental booth at the airport, but Richard was a good-natured soul and apparently hadn't minded the thought of the trip. Perhaps he had looked forward to a few hours of the uncomplicated and wholly superficial flirtation their relationship had fallen into.

She would never know for sure, for as she paused just outside the departure gate he was nowhere to be found.

Damn the man, she thought without heat, for he was a talented actor but as frivolous as he was good-natured, and no doubt the arrangements they'd made had slipped his light-hearted mind.

She pivoted on one sandalled heel, intent on renting a car, and nearly collided into the hard, relaxed body that had strolled up behind her.

Few men could make her head tilt back. She was at an equal level with Richard, though slender as a reed against his muscled handsomeness. But this man she had to look up to; she'd had to from the very beginning.

Her sensual mouth tightened at her inward lurch of recognition, but the undisciplined words escaped her anyway. 'What the hell are you doing here?'

Adam smiled, and reached to take her case from her nerveless fingers with a sculpted hand. He was as cool as ever, the grey eyes aloof and hooded, his lean expression composed. He was dressed in tight faded jeans and a light summer shirt with the sleeves rolled to the elbows. The outfit was unpretentious and unaffected, and emphasised the bulky curvature of his chest and arms, the heavy bulge of powerful thighs, the long, evocative line of his unbelted waist. His body was that of a stunningly magnificent animal, and his mind that of an unbreached treasure vault; dear God, he was so intensely alive and sexually vibrant and torturously distant.

'Hello to you too, darling,' he purred with an imperturbably sardonic note. 'Yes, I had a good weekend, thank you. How was never-never land?'

Her breath hissed between her teeth. Had she been restrained these last two weeks? Had she ever managed such an impossibility around him? Well, it was gone, all of it; blown to smithereens in the winter storm-blast of his impenetrable eyes.

'What have you done with Richard?' she enunciated in icy wrath.

'I tied him up and left him on the nearest railroad tracks, of course,' he said as he gave her a very odd look. 'Why, do you fancy playing the rescuing heroine? I should warn you that he'll be fickle with his gratitude—the love of his life is whoever happens to be with him at the moment.'

She had matched him stride for stride towards the short-term car park without even thinking about it. Now she stopped dead in the middle of crossing a car lane, her clenched fists rigid at her sides and her eyes closed tight. Her temper was an evil genius, and she was determined not to misplace it; it belonged right where she had put it, a hard, coiled lump of burning heat in her breast.

A taxi roared up to her, screamed to a stop, and the driver found his car horn and leaned on it rudely.

'Yvonne, you're blocking the traffic,' remarked Adam in mild warning.

Her body quivered, then she whirled, long legs ravening the short distance to the taxi. The driver watched in escalating amazement as she jerked the sunglasses off her nose, and thrust her furious face through his open window. Her deadly gaze bored into his, and she growled very softly, 'Take that hand off your horn, or I shall be all too happy to do it for you.'

The man melted all over his seat, mouth gaping and shutting like a stranded fish. 'My God,' he gasped rapturously, 'aren't you—aren't you—you are, aren't you? Yvonne Trent, I love your films; my God—oh, I'm so sorry I was so rude, my wife is going to die—could you possibly, I mean, could I possibly have your autograph?'

Weren't taxi drivers supposed to be unforgivably belligerent and rude? She pulled back and leaned her forehead with resignation against the top of the window, for she'd been looking for a fight and felt bitterly disappointed.

The driver scrabbled for pen and paper with shaking hands and thrust it at her; she scribbled a charming note, signed it, and handed it back. By the end of the brief exchange, the man would have been happy to drive her anywhere on the continent, never mind about his wife. She turned away from his ecstatic face, the pleasant smile she'd adopted falling away from her to reveal a dark thundercloud.

Adam appeared to be quite relaxed. His powerful body leaned indolently against a nearby concrete pillar. The long hand he ran through his wine-red hair hid his face from her. She frowned and stalked over to him, and hesitated as she caught a glimpse of his gleeful eyes. 'What happened to you?'

He shook his head, averted his face, and explained with deceptive calm, 'Swallowed wrong.'

Her eyes narrowed in suspicion, the unwilling question dragged from her lips. 'Are you all right?'

His nod was enthusiastic, and she heaved a great, long-suffering sigh. Lord, she would never understand him,

never in a million years; she shouldn't even try to, it was
a foregone conclusion, but, instead of feeling peaceful
fatalism at the thought, she felt suddenly very
discouraged.

Adam's 'recovery' was too masterful. It was a pity.
She would have enjoyed pounding hard on his wide back.
He captured her slender shoulders with one hard, long
arm, and prompted her in the right direction. His eyes
were still sparkling with a gigantic remnant of some
strange reaction, but the tough precision of his handsome
expression was once again composed.

She preferred him debilitated, and frowned her dis-
pleasure as she probed, 'Are you sure you're all right?'

'Perfectly sure,' replied Adam with a slight smile. He
glanced at her and then said a bizarre thing. 'Yvonne,
you are exquisite.'

Her gaze startled very wide. She thrust her dark glasses
back on her face to hide it, muttering shakenly, 'Oh,
please.'

He let her go to unlock the door of the BMW they
had halted by. It was his car; he must have driven it
through the desert.

Her imagination saw him speeding along the open
straight road at night, solitary and withdrawn and
spearheaded with twin pin-points of light. She slid into
her seat as he held the door, a weak surrender of boneless
muscles at the thought of his long hands negligent on
the steering-wheel, his body relaxed, that king's face in
repose, the elegant line of his mouth stern with thought-
fulness, and remote.

He slid into the driver's seat, put on his seatbelt and
started the car. Only then did he look at her troubled
expression, a quick, light-filled, unrevealing glance.

'You are exquisite,' he repeated with a cool deliberation that had a shattering effect. 'Even in the midst of your most terrible temper, you still find room to be generous, still manage to cloak the harsh emotions that prey upon you, still manage to protect other people's vulnerabilities from what you think is the worst part of yourself.'

She covered her face with one hand and turned away from him. She couldn't help it. 'I haven't the faintest idea what you're talking about,' she whispered unsteadily.

'You're a liar,' he said, ruthless in his understanding. 'You lie to me, but you lie to yourself most of all. I find I much prefer the honesty of your fury.'

'Damn you,' she gritted. Her hands, lying impotent in her lap, clenched and unclenched. 'Why are you doing this?'

If he was an amazement before, at least he didn't fail to continue living up to expectations.

'I told Richard I'd come pick you up because I wanted us to have a chance to talk in private,' said Adam briefly, frowning in concentration as he negotiated through the city traffic with swift, decisive driving, just as he did everything else.

'Whatever happened to saying please?' she snapped.

'You would have said no,' he said in a frigid voice. 'I know you that well, at least. God knows, you don't grant any quarter or opportunity. The only way I seem to be able to get any time alone with you is by taking you captive, by forcing it, by stealing the bits of you that you're careless enough to leave exposed, and damn, but that's not an occurrence that happens often. You're my weak link, and I'm concerned about you.'

'Weak link!' she exclaimed in horror and revulsion. The hurt was appalling, both to her pride and to her self-confidence. 'How can you say that to me? My professionalism is perfect!'

'Oh, yes,' he murmured, and at first it was a quiet, angry sound, 'perfection. That must be important to you. Do you want to hear it? Very well: your technique is flawless. Unescapably. You have Richard, Rochelle and Sally and even your own father in awe of you. You're never late, you never miss a cue, never screw up your lines. You blow up at the drop of a hat at any other time, but you never lose your temper on the job when they do. You're patient, you improvise beautifully to cover their inadequacies, and even in exhaustion you're just so perfect.'

'Then for God's sake why are you shouting at me?' she cried furiously, holding her clenched fists to her pounding forehead. He was attacking her without mercy, without warning, and her eyes were hunted and wild with provocation.

'Because I hate it,' he said from between gritted teeth, and for once the line of his mouth was not cut in elegance, but primal, twisted, volatile. 'Because you're not *giving* anything to your performance, and you're *giving* all the wrong things to everyone else. You do everything I tell you, take every direction without a murmur—you're like a human doll, flesh and blood and no spirit. It's almost pornographic.'

'I have never in my life been spoken to the way you speak to me,' snarled Yvonne, her eyes filled with furious tears. Furious tears, no technique or manipulation, but the real thing; she hadn't cried in sincerity in front of another human being in so many years, she'd lost count.

Her fists uncurled, fingers going to her cheeks to touch the wetness. She looked at her damp fingertips in astonishment. He did this to her. 'How dare you call me pornographic? My God, it's outrageous, you throwing stones. You're the one who bought me; well, my friend, I guess I've learned a pretty lesson these last few weeks. Everyone has a price, but let the buyer beware, because he gets only what he pays for.'

'I didn't pay for this.' He said it with such contempt, with such underlying emotion that had she granted him the ability to express it she would have called it pain. 'What happened to you? When you fought me, we had something to work with, but you changed the rules somewhere along the way. Where have you gone these last two weeks?'

'Nowhere, nowhere at all,' she said wearily, tired of struggling against his goads and her own terrifying emotions. 'Adam, it's all in your head.'

He made a sound of pure rage, and the glance he speared her with was electrifying as he said with incredulity, 'The worst part about it is that nobody else seems to notice it. You've locked yourself away and hidden the key, and you could conceivably sail through any awards ceremony on the basis of the performance you're giving now. But, sweetheart, you and I would both know it would be a travesty. My God, winning an award wouldn't even be an injustice, because without even trying, without even pushing yourself, you are the best actress I've ever seen.'

'Praise from Caesar?' The viciousness slipped out, in spite of herself, stabbing him, stabbing her. Her breath sucked in; she held it tight, and in her pounding breast her coiled temper reared back and raised its head.

'I'm not giving you praise.' The harsh whisper could have been a lion's roar and it would have had the same effect. She flinched, and missed the quickening of his sharp attention at her malicious rejoiner, the silent menace of his hawkish gaze spearing in with shotgun focus. 'I'm too offended to give you praise.'

'You're too offensive for me to accept it, even if you were,' she snarled back, holding on to her seat tight just in case she rocketed off it with the force of her own emotion. Her temper hissed, snake-like, and struck. 'You rummage around in our heads like a kid playing dress-up in an attic: try this emotion on, try that. It's all so intellectual for you, isn't it? How to put the puzzle pieces together in the best possible way! How to capture us on film—your words: "capture", "steal", "take"! Well, I won't be taken!'

He said, his face bloodless, 'So you really are angry with me still. You didn't go away, or curl up and die inside that body after all. I wondered.'

'I'm cursed with a long attention-span,' she spat.

'You must be, because I swear your anger at me has been years in building up.'

At first she couldn't believe she heard it, and gasped, 'What?'

'You heard me,' he growled, and the midnight-red fall of his hair on to that strong, golden forehead was only a visible manifestation of the molten lava that poured from him then, both psychic and physical. How could she have ever compared him to a white snowfall in winter? He radiated volcanic heat. 'You're so patho-logically determined not to lose yourself the way you did the last time. How insecure can you get? I'm the villain in this piece, the ravager and the taker, in a B-movie retake of all the injuries that happened to you before.'

'You swore that you'd never bring that up again!' she snarled in rage. 'Damn you, you promised me!'

His eyebrows, dark and sleek and dusted with fire, shot up in classic satirical astonishment. 'I would have been more than happy to leave the past where it belongs,' he snapped furiously. 'But it wouldn't stay there, would it, Yvonne? It had to raise its ugly head in your mind, and suddenly the face of the past has become mine! Well, I won't play the role you've forced on me! I'll challenge, and goad, and say whatever damned thing I please to you, but I will not suck your soul dry, not for this film or for any reason, and you'll have to come to terms with it!'

She was stunned; to the bottom of her intense, fierce, confused soul, she was stunned, and she subsided into reeling silence. Had she really cast Adam in her mind into such a repressive and dominating role? Had she unconsciously been expecting him to drain her of every aspect of her individuality? Had her fear of self-change transmuted into such a paranoia?

She twisted her restless body in her seat, staring at him, at the ferocious lowering of his brows, the skin covering his cheekbones taut and darkened, his mouth twisted and tight, his beautiful hands on the steering-wheel snarled with frustration.

A light bulb went off in her head. The Iceman was every bit a façade as anything an actor had ever produced; Adam was an actor still, playing the cool, unruffled part of the leader for the people who needed guidance; wearing serenity as easily and as well as he wore designer clothes.

With her, however, he took the gloves off. With her, he gave as good as he got, unstintingly, furiously, unshielding the nuclear blast of his own powerful personality to tower in his brilliance and his own glee.

Just as she had never pulled any punches with him, or tried to avert the furnace of her heated temper but threw it at him without reservation. All of it. Without diminishment or being destroyed, in fierce exhilaration.

The things she had thought she knew about men had been why she'd chosen with such cold-blooded determination to slap Adam's face the first time she'd met him, for she had thought, mistakenly, that his male ego would never be able to survive the injury to his reputation and his pride. Instead he had stood unflinching and faced her down and won the day in a good, clean fight. Perhaps the honour in it had been a little tarnished, but Yvonne found she wasn't bothered at all by a little tarnished honour. Heaven only knew, hers wasn't immaculate.

She looked out at the passing flat, desert-shrubbed scenery and thought it was the most transcendent expression of respect she had ever experienced. Adam found her a worthy opponent, worthy enough to shout at, worthy enough to shed his cool façade and show her who he really was.

'Now what are you thinking?' he sighed wearily, and in her hypersensitive state she thought she felt him brace himself.

'I'm thinking,' she said slowly, 'that I owe you an apology.'

The very quality of the frozen silence emanating from him was a statement of the depth of his surprise.

'What for?' he said then, sounding almost bored.

She didn't believe what she heard. He wasn't bored, for the incredible heat was still radiating from him; he was as tense as a high strung stallion ready to kick out and rear in screaming defiance. 'For being a liar,' she replied wryly, and she laid her head back against her seat. 'For lying to you, but lying to myself most of all.'

After a moment, Adam said in a very quiet voice, 'Thank you.'

Her head rolled on the head-rest and she looked at him and whispered, 'I'm scared of losing myself. I'm scared that if it happens this time I may never find myself again.'

She saw a muscle in his lean jaw flex once, spasmodically, and he unclenched one of his fists to grope for her hand, and to hold it hard. 'Do you know what I think?' he said, his tone still very quiet but underlaid with a savage bite. 'I think you were unfortunate enough to be surrounded by selfish, greedy people that last year you acted who didn't care about human cost as long as they achieved the end product. Anyone with an ounce of sensitivity can recognise someone on the brink. All they had to do was reach out a hand and pull you back.'

'Who knows? Maybe you're right.' She gave a shrug, and then simply amazed herself by saying, in pain, 'I'm sorry I'm not the quality of actress you wanted.'

His intake of breath was as sharp and unshielded as if she'd laid into him with a whip. Then he said harshly, 'It doesn't matter, not any more.'

She regarded him in bewilderment. It had mattered enough for him to shout at her. 'It matters to me.'

'Then don't let it. Listen to me talk about insensitive louts, when I've been the biggest one of all,' he said, managing to gentle himself as he felt her confusion. He sent her a brief, frowning glance. 'Yvonne, you decide what you want to bring to the film. The technique will be quite enough if that is what you choose. To do any better, you would have to lose yourself; a true actor becomes his part, not merely plays it. That's a leap of faith from you that I haven't got the right to demand.'

She closed her eyes and shook all over her body, vibrating under his strong, warm hand, which tightened in silent reaction.

He was a man who would always live by his own dictates as long as others allowed him to, and then he would be as stern and as mercilessly impartial as a judge. And he had promised her that he would not push her beyond her own limits, and she had told him, in truth that time, in harshest unforgiving self-truth, that he wouldn't have to, for she managed it quite well enough on her own.

She had done it before, hadn't she? She had been Celeste, Mary, Elizabeth . . .

'What if I try?' she whispered.

Unseen, unfelt by her, his chest moved hard. 'If you would try,' murmured Adam, his body rigid, 'if you would trust me that far, I would bring you back to yourself.'

'You would?' She opened her eyes.

His face was rock-hard with assurance. 'Every time, Yvonne.'

A sense of wonderment stole over her. Dear God help her, she believed him.

He signalled and turned the car down a dusty dirt road that they followed for a few miles until they came upon the location site; she recognised the immense cluster of trucks bearing the studio logo, and the trailers where the cast and crew would live for the duration of the filming.

Off to one side, by a lazy thread of river and a copse of trees, green and lush in the dry bowl of land, was the house and outbuildings that was the movie set.

She stared at it, drawn by a copper-tasting sense of excitement and fear. Adam pulled the BMW to a halt, the powerful car engine idling, and looked at her.

'Don't trust me blindly,' he said with a suddenness that shocked her, his grey eyes devouring every nuance of her expressive face. 'Put me to the test. A very small one.'

She swallowed drily as she looked at him, and hesitated. He was waiting, vivid and intent and the only thing real, in the drowsy heat of the early Arizona evening. She plunged. 'All right.'

He gunned the car in swift, abrupt reaction, and the BMW raced towards the movie set. Yvonne breathed in hard, and held it, and gritted her teeth as they came to a stop near the quiet, waiting house. Her terror and her eagerness would not let her wait for him to come to her, and they both climbed out of the car at the same time, and he walked over to her and stopped at her side, and watched.

It was up to her.

In typical impetuous fashion, she turned and ran home. Up the wooden steps, through the unlocked door and into the front room.

It was eerily familiar. It would be already, for she had seen the sketches of the set designs. She whirled through the rooms, touching things, putting them down. Her things, in the bedroom; her hairbrush, and shabby mirror. A few ribbons. She opened the wardrobe and looked in. Her clothes.

Hannah sat on her bed, and breathed deeply. The quiet of the day stole into her limbs. An unobtrusive voice asked her from the doorway, 'What are you doing?'

'Dreaming,' said Hannah, who tilted back her chestnut head. Her lips pulled into a private, untouchable smile. 'I always dream in the afternoon. It's too hot to do anything else.'

'What are you dreaming about?' asked the quiet voice.

'Oh, fine things,' she whispered, and shook her head at the useless fancy. 'Servants, and a lovely ballgown, and a man to dance with me.'

'Your husband?'

Hannah laughed a little, a tired, gentle sound, and didn't answer. Her eyes opened suddenly, and she frowned in puzzlement at the evidence in the room around her. Then she leaped to her feet in agitation and hurried to straighten the room. The serenity her face had gained while she had sat dreaming fractured into delicate distress. It wasn't right, wasn't right.

'Now what are you doing?' asked the voice, patiently.

'I wouldn't do this,' said Hannah, who was upset by the disorder. 'I wouldn't leave my room like this. Everything has to be put away, in its place, everything has to be neat and tidy. There isn't any room for dreaming here. It makes a mess of your life. It makes you want things you can't have.'

'What else isn't right, Hannah?'

Everything was better now. She turned and walked out of the bedroom to look, and she hurried through the house rearranging, explaining as she went.

The kitchen had to be as spartan and as straight as the rest of the house, until she turned to the golden slant of the sun as it entered the window, and she stood slender as an arrow as dust motes danced around her body in a fairy waltz.

The man who had followed her like a fiery shadow stood and stared at the sight, transfixed.

She was unaware of him. She whispered, 'I'm going to lose it all, aren't I? Everything I loved, everything I've hoped and dreamed for, my father, no children, my husband whom I cannot love no matter how I try, my looks, my God, my face. This God-awful place will take my youth away.' She slumped in exhaustion, and her face slowly bent to her chest, and her massive eyes closed in eloquent despair.

Her unnoticed watcher, the man of legendary control, moved uncontrollably.

Almost immediately, Hannah straightened in her pride and pain, and whispered, 'It doesn't matter. I'm too busy for it to matter. Everything has to be put in its place.'

Gentle arms came around her. She started violently at the intrusion. Adam pulled her close, and held her hard, and his face came down to rest on the top of her drooping head. The sensual evidence of his touch was too powerful. She groaned as Hannah splintered.

'Enough,' he whispered. 'Yvonne, for pity's sake, that's enough.'

Yvonne lifted her head and looked at him. His grey eyes were wide. He was so beautiful, and so strong, and so impossible to deny, this man she had made Hannah dream about, who had danced with her under the moonlight. He seemed to be labouring under the influx of a powerful emotion.

'I'm back,' she said simply, and her expression transformed in exultant rediscovery.

'Oh, darling,' he said in a deep voice, and he held her fiercely. '*Well done!*'

It was the first praise he had offered her since they had started work together, and the ring of truth in it was unmistakable. Yvonne laid her head on his shoulder and was content.

CHAPTER FIVE

IT WAS the beginning of the second month, and the whirlwind machine had coalesced into the brilliant laser pin-point of one undeniable, inexorable man.

Nothing was good enough for him. He did not shout it, or explode into harsh impatience. He dictated in awesome, unrelenting quiet. Retake after retake. His cast struggled under the ruthless request for their highest performance, and gave him what he asked for. One soft-spoken word from him, and his crew leaped to obey.

The first few weeks were terribly exhausting for Yvonne, who had fallen out of the habit of remembering what a long day of filming could entail. Her private trailer became a haven that she stumbled into at night, to fall into bed and plunge into a deep, dreamless sleep. The days when she was actually acting started before dawn.

Her hair was washed and arranged, and she suffered under endless attention to the detail of her dress. Every aspect had to be correct in order to maintain veracity from one scene to the next, and, since they did not shoot in chronological order in the story but followed the best schedule for utilising personnel and times of day and special effects, that meant consulting long, detailed lists that were excruciatingly meticulate.

The first time Make-up had a go at her was an abysmal failure.

Adam took one look at her face, at the expert and delicate artifice that enhanced her already unique, adamant features into a stunning display. His face darkened. He roared, in an undiluted, rampant display of temper that was all the more terrifying for being so uncharacteristic.

'What the hell have they done to your face?'

She nearly leaped out of her skin. She shouted back, more startled than anything else, 'I haven't the faintest idea!'

He growled, low in his chest, his forceful features clenched into a scowl. Unbeknown to either of them, the busy crew going about their individual preparations for the day had halted and watched the heated interplay in immense fascination.

'Well, dammit, why didn't you pay attention to what they were doing to you?' he snapped, resting his fists on his lean hips and glaring at her. 'You're wrong, you're all wrong!'

Unconsciously she mimicked his stance, stood practically toe to toe with the man, thrust her angry face into his and snapped back, 'It's not my job to oversee Make-up!'

'No,' he said grimly, his grey eyes throwing bolts of silver lightning, 'it's your job to see that Hannah's character remains consistent. Can you honestly tell me that when you looked in the mirror you saw Hannah's face looking back at you?'

'I didn't look in a mirror!' she yelled furiously, glaring up at him. Where was the Iceman now, Yvonne? Where was his soft-spoken patience?

At her words, Adam's eyebrows shot up in incredulity. He stared at her as if he couldn't believe his ears, and laughed out loud, a short, disbelieving bark. 'You mean to tell me you didn't look in a mirror once this morning? My God, what kind of a woman are you?'

Her lush, subtly painted mouth fell open and she gasped audibly. 'I'm more woman than you'll ever get the opportunity to know, you insufferable man!' she raged, beside herself with fury at the perceived insult.

To her escalating amazement, Adam creased up. He laughed in uncontainable amusement, and she glared at him, and gnashed her teeth and wondered incoherently how she could strike back with enough force to knock that delighted smile off his handsome, infuriating face.

'What were you doing in Make-up all that time?' He was trying manfully to get a grip on himself. 'Counting sheep?'

She nearly hit him. Her fist was curled, cocked back and thrumming with tension as she looked at the line of his lean jaw with narrowed eyes and thought of planting it there, right there. Oh, such a lovely thought. 'Mornings,' she said in a deadly voice, 'are not my best time of day.'

'Apparently not,' he remarked in derision. She nearly let fly with a right hook then, but his light gaze fell down the length of her taut, battle-ready stance. He looked at her fist, and said, 'Violence, my dear?'

She said from between her teeth, 'You do seem to ask for it. Why is it you always yell at me? You never shout at anybody else, although they tiptoe around you as if they half expect it—you only shout at me. Why, Adam, why?'

'I haven't the slightest inclination to yell at anyone else. You quite satisfactorily draw all my fire,' he purred with a tight, glittering smile.

He almost wanted her to do it. She could see that and wouldn't succumb, and forced her hand wide open, the long, narrow fingers stiff and taloned. She displayed her flat, empty palm to him in mockery and said with intimate malice, 'Sally's scared stiff of you.'

His beautiful eyes lifted to hers. They were afire. 'Sally,' murmured Adam with ineffable gentleness, 'isn't woman enough to stand up to me. You never did tell me.'

She glared at him blankly, not understanding why her chest had become so constricted she could hardly breathe. She was struggling and she didn't know why. 'Tell you what?'

'What you were thinking about when you were in Make-up?'

What in the world was he doing now? His persistence was as stubborn and as incomprehensible as anything she had ever witnessed. She finally got a deep breath into her restricted lungs, and the rushing intake of oxygen made her light-headed and dizzy.

'I wasn't thinking at all,' she grumbled, half embarrassed by the confession. 'I fell asleep.'

He roared again, this time in laughter. The sound produced in her a gut reaction. She wasn't even in conscious control of it. Her hand doubled into a fist again, and sprang upwards—and was caught at hip level, in a lightning-swift movement from him that she hadn't even seen.

He held her effortlessly and seemed to recall where they were. He looked around them and caught sight of their silent audience, who hadn't heard anything but the loudest of the shouted exchange but were watching the unfolding drama with absorption all the same.

He said to the crew very softly, 'Don't you all have jobs that need to be done?'

Indeed they did, and they remembered that fact with great alacrity. Yvonne felt shaken free of some sorcerous enchantment, and blinked rapidly at the return of sanity. She tried to twist out of Adam's grip, but the movement only served to draw his attention back to her.

He frowned critically down at her and strode towards the make-up caravan, dragging her along with him. Just once, she thought with longing, her legs flashing swiftly to keep up with his longer stride. Just once she wondered what it would be like to be invited, instead of hauled about like a sack of potatoes, or a battered stuffed toy dragged along in a small boy's wake.

But at that thought she frowned, and her plaintive little fantasy blew up in her face. Adam was as far from the image of a small boy as chalk was from cheese; he was all man, hard and muscled and sinuous with graceful virility. And if he invited her, what would she do? Would she refuse him contrarily, or would she accept?

Would she?

He stalked up the narrow metal-framed steps, entered the caravan without knocking, and she scrambled along behind him. The make-up artist turned in surprise. Adam ignored the other woman and thrust Yvonne towards the large lit mirror and said tersely, 'Look at yourself.'

She threw a scowl at him for the sake of principle, then turned to stare at her reflection. She couldn't seem to concentrate on her own image, however, and her gaze went to the tall, auburn-haired, golden visage of the man who stood at her shoulder. Was that how other people saw them when they were together—her own slender body brought to intense femininity by the brooding power of his masculine presence?

'Do you see what I see?' he asked after a moment, and she shook her head in numb incomprehension. She didn't dare tell him what she saw; she could hardly dare to admit it to herself.

'What do you see?' she whispered through dry lips.

His reflection smiled at her. He said quietly, 'I see fine things. I see servants, a ballgown, a man to dance with. You're astonishingly beautiful this way, proud and far too aristocratic. You're undeniably and irrefutably Yvonne, but not Hannah.'

For the first time she really focused on herself, and understood, and nodded.

Adam said to the make-up artist, 'I want her naked.'

The stark words were like a blow to her unsuspecting solar plexus.

Sheer shock quivered over her face, and she stood unmasked before him and before herself, but his attention was mercifully on the other woman. What did this evidence tell her?

The internal crisis was too much, the revelation too exposed to the raw, hot-lit air. She shut down all systems, closed her eyes, stood like a statue and refused to know.

The conversation between Adam and the make-up artist continued over her unnoticed silence. He was saying, 'No, not even so much as a dusting of powder. Nothing, I tell you—the camera close-ups would pick it up. Her skin is fine and flawless enough. It's not often we get a chance to take advantage of such incredible natural beauty, and I intend to make the most of it. Wash it all off, and be quick about it; we start shooting in fifteen minutes.'

'Yes, sir,' said the artist.

Adam made a move as if to go, then his glance fell on her frozen stance, and he hesitated. 'Yvonne? What's the matter?'

He sounded preoccupied, impatient, ready to get on with the long, bruising schedule of the day.

She whispered through bloodless lips, 'Nothing. Just go away.'

She had shut herself blind in the dark confinement of her soul

She didn't see the expression in his grey eyes as he stood just behind her shoulder, staring at her, not touching her—almost touching her, as his hand came up to halt in the air just above the unchecked chestnut fall of her hair. The masculine hand clenched into a fist and he looked terrifying with ruthless intent, the hair falling in searing, untamed fire on to his brow, the expression on his hawkish face insatiable and atavistic. He looked predatory, poised on the brink of falling ravenously upon her.

The make-up artist was witness to it all and her mouth fell open in a silent gasp. Adam's ferocious gaze shot to the other woman. He lifted up a pre-emptory finger at her and shook his head warningly, and she nodded in vigorous response. Then he pivoted, an extraordinarily neat movement in such a confined space, and left.

Yvonne relaxed bonelessly as she heard the door of the caravan shut. She would have brooded then, in smoky swirling terror, except that her attention was snagged on a very odd occurrence.

The make-up artist, heretofore a voluble and gossipy individual, was completely reticent. She creamed Yvonne's face and wiped away all traces of the make-up with a light, deft touch that would not redden her fine-grained skin, and she did it all without saying a single word.

Yvonne watched her in mild puzzlement. She would almost have believed that the other woman was a different person entirely, had she not the evidence of her own eyes.

Could things go from bad to worse, when they had started out so very badly?

The dispute over her make-up—or lack of it—had happened on her very first day of filming, and that had been over two weeks ago. Since then the atmosphere between her and the winter king fulminated with impending crisis.

She didn't understand it, refused to think about it, was damned if she would obsess any more over inexplicabilities, her own most of all. She wasn't in the State of Arizona any longer; she was in a state of denial, and as she adjusted to the demands made upon her she threw herself into her work with heedless, extravagant passion, and when she wasn't working she was mightily, dangerously bored.

She was her own worst enemy when she engaged in stress-related behaviour.

If hell was a place with absolutely nothing to do, then they were in the very pit of it. The nearest civilisation was a sleepy little town in the throes of shock over the flamboyant arrival of the film crew, who were under strict orders to be on their best behaviour in public.

Once one toured the tiny post office and the grocery store, which carried everything from food, medicines and paperbacks to magazines and newspapers and doubled as the local bag and feed centre for the farmers, there were only two other places to go, the bars in cut-throat competition with each other and located at opposite ends of town.

Yvonne had prowled through it all, including the bars. She bought paperbacks and newspapers, aspirins, made friends with the locals, had two beers, one in each bar, and got invited to several different homes for a variety of reasons both reputable and disreputable. She turned down family dinners and the other, more unorthodox offers with the same practised, unperturbed charm.

That killed one afternoon dead.

Then she turned her attention to the film cast and crew. Sally, her 'sister' in the film, and she had become good friends, much as she had predicted they would. They had managed to do so by virtue of the fact that they had absolutely nothing in common with each other. Rochelle, her 'mother', was a tough nut that didn't want to be cracked; Yvonne left the older woman alone. Her relationship with her father Christopher was already intimate with a lifetime of loving familiarity. Richard was Richard, and as such didn't merit more than a fragment of her restless, hungry attention.

The crew, however, had some merit. One particular special effects fellow, Jerry, she had already met some years ago. He was excellent at his job, and under-utilised at the moment since the film didn't call for many effects, a scamp of the first order, and as bored as she was; Yvonne was delighted to renew his acquaintance.

They fell into an argument one sultry afternoon, and, since there was nothing better to do, Jerry offered to take her out in his battered car to prove his point.

She agreed enthusiastically but wanted to drive. That was good for another argument. They climbed into his Chevy and took off down the dirt road, and when they reckoned they were far enough away and downwind from the film site to avoid disrupting the shoot Jerry pulled off the road with a clattering bump.

Then he proceeded to teach her how to do doughnuts. He was right, too: they didn't need an icy pavement to do it on. Yvonne hung on to her seatbelt for dear life and shouted with glee. The body of the car was a hopeless mess, but Jerry kept the engine in beautiful condition. They roared over the bumpy ground, and twisted and flung about, and it was better than a carnival ride. Then she managed to persuade him to let her try, and took the wheel, and within minutes was flinging the car around in circles with the expertise of a professional.

Jerry shouted that he was impressed. Yvonne grinned and yelled her thanks.

A rock shot up and shattered the windscreen.

The transparent glass exploded into opaque, spider-webbed white. Instantly she jammed both feet on clutch and brake for a precipitate emergency stop, even though she knew intellectually that they were probably quite safe, for there wasn't anything in the flat desert-like expanse for them to hit, except for more rocks and dirt. The sharp screeching halt of the car brought the shattered glass down on them, in a brilliant sun-sparkled cascade.

'Nice reflexes,' said Jerry in the ensuing silence.

She shot him a repentant glance. 'Oh, I'm so sorry. I'll buy you another.'

'Another car?' he asked.

The delighted incredulity in his dancing eyes made her burst out laughing. She was still laughing, an infectious,

light-hearted sound, as she climbed out of the car with
extreme care, scattering false diamonds generously with
each slight movement.

They were both preoccupied with inspecting the
damage done to the car. Neither one was prepared when
the wrath of God descended upon them.

'I have never in my life seen such criminal, irrespon-
sible behaviour,' said the lethal quiet voice from behind
her.

Jerry had the advantage. He was on the opposite side
of the car and all he had to do was look up. Yvonne
jumped a good foot into the air and landed facing the
most furious man she had ever seen in her life.

She had witnessed Adam angry before. Adam beside
himself with rage was like nothing she had ever before
experienced.

He was dead white, down to the taut, twisted snarl of
his lips, and his eyes were glazing beacons in that rigid,
awesome mask. He was breathing hard, and must have
raced like a madman from the dirt road where he had
left his BMW slewed to one side, the driver's door still
flung open. She fell back an instinctive step as he strode
over to her, and tilted up her chin with gentle fingers
that shook.

Those terrible eyes ravaged her face. 'Are you hurt?'
he murmured almost absently. 'Cut anywhere?'

She shook her head numbly in a sprinkling downfall
of glass splinters. She looked like a dusty, dishevelled
elfin queen, a proud creature born of the summer wind,
and sunshine adored her long, graceful body in sparkling,
incandescent brilliance.

Adam detonated. He roared deep-throated at Jerry,
who flinched as if he'd been shot. The subject matter

was disjointed; it had something to do with retribution, and lawsuits, and imminent death, and the force of it distended the powerful tendons in his neck.

Shaken and astonished, she tried to stem the flood, to calm the raging beast. 'Adam,' she said with an attempt at calm.

Apparently he couldn't hear her over the noise he was making, and so she raised her voice. 'Adam?'

He started to round the front of the Chevy. Dear God, it looked as if he meant to throttle the other man. She screamed ear-splittingly at the top of her lungs. '*Adam*!'

Well, that got his attention, at least. He looked at her with silver-shot, blinded eyes and shouted hoarsely, 'What—damn it?'

Once he'd focused on her, however, she wished she had kept her mouth shut, but it was too late now, and she would die before she backed down. She cleared her throat and asked tentatively, 'Er—what are you doing away from the shoot?'

His hand shot out in a wide sweeping arc. The movement had the savagery of a lion striking with outstretched claws. 'Chasing the path of your fall-out, what else?' he bit out.

She looked up in concern, as did Jerry. The dark cloud of dust they'd stirred up hung lazily in the air, an ominous yellow-tinged spiral, but it had gone nowhere near the movie set. She considered pointing that fact out to him, but felt he might not be in the mood to appreciate it.

Instead she said with the sweet voice of reason, 'Well, at any rate, stop taking it out on Jerry. He was only teaching me how to do doughnuts. I was the one who was driving.'

'God give me strength,' he whispered. Then, without looking at the other man, he told Jerry flatly, 'Get out of here.'

Jerry climbed into the Chevy and got. Adam turned the ungovernable vitriol of his rage on to her. 'You stupid woman, don't you know what damage you could have done to yourself? You could have been scarred for life—you could have been blinded——'

'Well, I wasn't, was I?' she exclaimed, her eyes very wide. Inwardly she was terrified at being left alone with him this way. Thinking to lighten the fearfully dangerous moment, she gave him a quick grin and shrugged, her hands outstretched, and said merrily, 'Besides, I'm insured.'

Wrong.

He made a strangled, inarticulate sound at the back of his throat, took two great strides towards her, fastened his greedy hands on to her shoulders in total disregard for the danger that he might cut himself, and he shook her. Hard, long, and continuously.

She bowed before his fury, flinging her narrow hands out to grasp the tight bulge of his biceps, devastated at the actuality of his physical release, and her own total helplessness in the face of it. The world tilted, and nothing was sane, and a cry broke from her parted lips.

He stopped, and hauled her without mercy against the ungiving hardness of his chest and snarled in a low monotone that was even more terrible than his previous shouting had been, 'So you're bloody insured, are you? I'm sure it would be a consolation to your parents had that damned car rolled over and you'd been crushed to death.'

Her gaze widened even further as she felt the tremor that shot through his strong body, and she wondered with deep, self-inflicted bitterness just how stupid she could possibly get.

He'd actually been afraid; that was fear for her screaming at the heart of his fury and violence, and everything she had said to him had been absolutely the worst possible thing to say.

She lifted an unsteady hand and laid it along his face. He had been so intent on snarling at her that he hadn't seen it coming, and he flinched reactively when her fingers touched his overheated skin. 'Adam,' she said, and for this one man in such a state she was gentle. 'It was an accident. Nobody was hurt. We were sensible, wore our seatbelts, and we were enjoying ourselves, and it—just—happened.'

'Sensible,' he repeated grimly, then he uttered a foul expletive.

But he was still at last, and listening. And wonder followed upon wonder; first she discovered gentleness, and now she found patience. She pointed out quietly, her great eyes searching his, 'Windscreens shatter all the time on the open highway from rocks thrown up by passing trucks. We weren't even doing twenty-five miles an hour, and there was nothing for us to run into.'

'You don't know what it looked like,' he said harshly, his mouth twisted. 'The car was whipping about, the engine roaring. Then I heard a horrible sound, a great loud crack, followed by the scream of brakes, and the whole car seemed to disappear into the great gusts of dirt billowing from the rear tyres. Damn it, Yvonne, I couldn't see what had happened.'

'My God,' she said, appalled, and then sighed in remorse. 'I'm sorry. It must have looked awful.'

He held her stare and said deliberately, 'It took ten years off my life.'

She was hardly aware of how her fingers stroked his cheek, and how his expression had softened because of it. 'All I can say is that we never dreamed we'd have an audience. We couldn't know you'd be watching.'

'No,' he agreed reluctantly, 'you couldn't know. Don't do it again?'

She shook her head without hesitation, and never even panicked or was the slightest bit concerned at how she was allowing another's fears to govern her behaviour. 'I won't,' she told him. 'I promise.'

He stared at her, in a long, searching silence, and finally the tension left his long body and he sighed. All of a sudden, he looked very weary. 'That'll have to do, I guess. Come on, then. Let's get you back and cleaned up before you do serious injury to yourself.'

Brought back to realisation of the circumstances, she looked down at herself and was even more appalled. She'd had no idea she was so covered in glass, and Adam had held her without regard. Why, he could have been cut just by touching her. Her flattened hands went out to brush down his front, but he swiftly forestalled her with a warning shake of his head.

'Splinters,' he said, ruefully.

Another thought had already occurred to her. She froze, and one stealthy hand tried to creep up to her head, but he caught it and forced it down again.

Then, of course, she knew, but she had to ask the horrified question anyway. 'I have the glass in my hair, don't I?'

GET 4 BOOKS A CUDDLY TEDDY AND A MYSTERY GIFT

Return this card, and we'll send you 4 Mills & Boon Temptations, absolutely FREE! We'll even pay the postage and packing for you!

We're making you this offer to introduce to you the benefits of Mills & Boon Reader Service: FREE home delivery of brand-new Temptation romances, at least a month before they're available in the shops, FREE gifts and a monthly Newsletter packed with offers and information.

Accepting these FREE books places you under no obligation to buy, you may cancel at any time, even after receiving just your free shipment.

Yes, please send me 4 free Mills & Boon Temptations, a cuddly teddy and a mystery gift as explained above. Please also reserve a Reader Service subscription for me. If I decide to subscribe, I shall receive 4 superb new titles every month for just £7.80 postage and packing free. If I decide not to subscribe I shall write to you within 10 days. The free books and gifts will be mine to keep in any case. I understand that I am under no obligation whatsoever. I may cancel or suspend my subscription at any time simply by writing to you.

4A4T

Ms/Mrs/Miss/Mr _____

Address _____

_____

_____ Postcode_____

Signature_____
I am over 18 years of age.

Get 4 books
a cuddly teddy and
mystery gift FREE!

SEE BACK OF CARD FOR DETAILS

No
stamp
needed

Mills & Boon Reader Service,
FREEPOST
P.O. Box 236
Croydon
CR9 9EL

Offer expires 31st October 1994. One per household. The right is reserved to refuse an
application and change the terms of this offer. Offer applies to U.K. and Eire only. Offer not
available for current subscribers to Mills & Boon Temptations. Readers overseas please
send for details. Southern Africa write to: IBS Private Bag X3010, Randburg 2125. You
may be mailed with offers from other reputable companies as a result of this application.

If you would prefer not to receive such offers, please tick this box. ☐

'All through it,' he agreed, and paused to regard her dismayed expression with something perversely like satisfaction.

Her dark gaze turned to him in anguished entreaty. She breathed, 'Oh, God, how will I get it all out?'

Adam threaded his fingers through hers, and led her towards his car. Somewhere along the line his uncontrolled rage had completely died away; somewhere between that moment, and the molten time when he had shaken her, some synchronous chain of events had eased the raging inferno.

He was serene again, and unhurried, and he told her in a soothing voice, 'Don't worry, I'll take care of it.'

'But how?' she cried, half wailed.

'Yvonne,' said the winter king with a stern and darkling glance, 'trust me.'

CHAPTER SIX

'TRUST me,' he'd said, and by so doing started a subterranean chain reaction inside of her that was unstoppable.

What happened was that he escorted her to the passenger side of the BMW, took a blanket from the boot of the car, shook it out and placed it on the seat and then placed her on the blanket and drove her back to her trailer.

Once there, he told her to wait outside, and Yvonne did so numbly. Then he went inside and came back out a few moments later with a bath-towel and a brush. The bath towel he wrapped carefully around her head in a turban; the brush he used all down the length of her body.

He attacked her with gusto. She was buffeted by the long, brisk swipes, barely keeping to her feet, and she yowled like a wounded cat at the indignity. Adam laughed at her sound and fury and swept her all the harder. It signified nothing.

It was all surface noise.

What really happened was internal and frightening. She studied him through her lashes covertly, noting the play of the early evening sunshine along the fluid, sculpted shift of muscles of his body, the shift of light and shadow that made his grey eyes so lucid and changeable, the deep fire of his auburn hair that was at such odds with the antique, hammered gold of his stern, handsome face.

When he had cleaned her up to his satisfaction, he stopped and leaned back, his hands thrust negligently into his trouser pockets.

'OK,' he said, and considered her with a thoughtful frown.

She appeared to recover her equilibrium and glared at him warily. It was all an act. It was all spitfire and shadows, and the classic misdirection of a magic show. Please don't let him look and really see her. Let him see the rabbit out of the hat; let him look on the façade and applaud and be satisfied with it; let the shabby performing clown go unnoticed.

He was telling her, 'Don't touch your hair now. Leave it wrapped in the towel while you strip out of those clothes and shower. I'm going to change as well, and I'll be back here in about ten minutes.'

She nodded, her expression serious and attentive. She really did it well.

His sharp gaze narrowed on her, and he remarked almost idly, 'I'd give anything to know what was going on behind those secretive eyes of yours.'

She froze, caught in the act, as it were, her audience unimpressed, the rabbit and the top hat vanishing in a puff of stage smoke.

'I don't know what you mean. Nothing's going on,' she told him, her chin tilted at a haughty angle, and only afterwards did she realise that she'd played the scene all wrong again, for she'd given herself away with the quick denial. She would have done far better simply to stare at him in incomprehension.

His slow, searing smile told her so. She closed her eyes at the failure, then turned to walk up the trailer steps.

'Yvonne,' said Adam, halting her escape into privacy. She looked over her shoulder at him enquiringly, one hand on the latch of the door. 'If I were you I would rinse off very well before I—soaped my body.'

Her bewildered lips parted at the words, so innocuous in meaning, so sultry in delivery. His hawkish eyes captured hers, and she caught fire. 'Because of the splinters,' he explained, in a murmurous verbal caress. 'Your skin is so much more delicate than mine.'

What was he saying to her? What was he communicating really? She promised, a shaken, fragile thread of sound, 'I'll—be careful.'

'Good,' he said very softly, intently, in full force and delicate focus. 'You see, I don't want you to cut yourself. I don't like you to be hurt, either mentally or physically.'

It was nothing, what he said. It was a product of re-action from the accident, a spoken acknowledgement of the fear that had propelled him, the inevitable lecture after the fact. She told herself so, but for some reason she couldn't make herself believe it, and she had to cover her face with one narrow, trembling hand, for he overwhelmed her.

And then, without ever having physically laid a hand on her, she felt the unbearable tension ease as he offered her release. 'I'll see you in a few minutes.'

Words were his multidimensional province; she was beyond them. She ran inside, stripped off her jeans and T-shirt in graceless haste, and flung herself into the tiny shower cubicle.

'Trust me,' he'd said, and she had, increasingly, over the weeks.

She had dive-bombed into his life, a falcon screaming for battle, and he had obliged her. He gave her every struggle she demanded, every opportunity to bristle, every reason to hurl her temper at him, and yet somehow he managed to become the victor. Somehow he managed to transmute their antagonistic relationship into a dynamic evolution.

Every ultimatum she had laid down for herself, every definitive stance, had been demolished. She would not act again—and now she did so. She would not be governed by another human being—but now she adapted her actions voluntarily at another's request. She would not be budged from her Montana ranch—and then she found herself, within a matter of weeks and much to her own surprise, in southern Arizona. She discovered gentleness, and patience, and they were as easy to incorporate as if they had always been there inside, waiting like flowering bulbs that slept in the ground during the winter only to unfurl at the first delicate sign of spring.

Hadn't she said that he would change her? Hadn't she warned herself that it would happen? Couldn't she gloat, morbidly, and flay herself with 'I told you so's?

But consider this: none of it felt alien. She hadn't lost herself in the changing; she had found that she was more than she'd ever imagined she could be. She was on an immense and wonderment-imbued quest of self-discovery, and what shook her to the core was that one single man, just one, as anchored and adamant as she and without domination, had impelled her to this.

Oh, she could cry from the terror. She lifted her face to the sharp sting of the shower spray and let it rain down on her.

They inhabited a transient world of falsity and illusion. The intensity of working on a movie produced deep creative bonds between people that felt transcendent at the time, but then, inevitably, it ended. The successful teams fractured; individuals shot off to other bondings and other horizons, and on the occasion when they met one another again it was often with remembered affection and delight. How good to see you again, what have you been doing with yourself—a new spouse, my God, kids?

So few bonds remained throughout the many separations and the lifestyles that spanned the globe; so few could be sustained under such a hectic pace. So many changes, so little to hold on to. Yvonne had learned not to hold on to anything but watch it all filter through her open fingers with wide, unflinching eyes. That was why she had been so resistant to self-change, for she was the only thing she'd allowed herself to rely upon, only she had remembered that fact far too late.

She shocked herself by sobbing aloud, a deep, physical, involuntary sound, her face contorted with anguish. She knew how to occupy the role of a graceful traveller through everyone's life but her own; her own, she didn't know what to do with.

'Trust me,' he'd said, and she did. But she didn't know the man she trusted. The evidence of him was everywhere around her, except for who he was, and she didn't know how to brace herself against the invisible umbilical cord that was strengthening between them, or how to prepare for the awful sense of loss when it ended.

The water in the shower ran cold. Yvonne shivered, and stood under it for as long as she could, for reasons she did not comprehend or wish to explore. When at last she could not stand it any longer, she turned it off and groped blindly for a clean towel to dry off with, her body shaking as if with palsy as she struggled into a thin cotton robe which she belted at her slim waist.

Movement sounded through the thin prefab walls of the trailer, and she exited the minuscule bathroom to find Adam in the kitchenette.

He had never been in her trailer before. He looked completely at ease and at home. He had showered as well, and was clad in a clean pair of jeans and a pale blue shirt that was carelessly untucked at the waist and unbuttoned. The smooth, wide, muscled chest that rippled with his every movement was a shocking exposure, and his sleek auburn hair was still wet.

She stopped dead at the first sight of him, the rigidity of her body a silent scream of protest, one hand clutching the neck of her robe together so tightly she almost strangled herself.

He glanced at her unsmilingly. He must have seen everything there was to see in that one comprehensive sweep of his eyes; he always did, and he never failed to comment on it.

'Go get your hairbrush,' he ordered softly. She went to her darkened bedroom and retrieved the brush from the bedside table, and got lost along the way. Oh, God, she couldn't face him. She clutched the brush to her chest and bowed her head over it, for the person she didn't trust was herself.

Adam said, from the doorway behind her, 'Lie down on the bed.'

The bow of her mouth was open, her eyes squeezed tight. She felt her extreme vulnerability, from her bare feet, to her state of undress, to her state of mind. She felt his imminent, watchful presence. Please, someone help her.

She went to the bed and lay on it. She heard him move then, in a subtle friction of cloth, and the light in the room came on, and she shut her eyes tighter and averted her face.

The man by the doorway stood and looked at the woman lying before him for long moments. He stared at the long reclining body, the lush, graceful swell of hips and breasts outlined against the lines of a robe that revealed more than it concealed, the half-exposed, slender, tanned legs, the intricate delicacy of her wrists and narrow hands, the hollows of her collarbones and throat, the angled line of her cheekbone and jaw.

For Yvonne the silent time felt like an eternity. She lay trembling and heated and completely devastated, knowing that he looked at her and saw what he saw, and she would have screamed had it been a release and had she had the strength for it.

Then he walked over, put his hands upon her, and guided her head to the side of the bed. He unwrapped the towel that had covered her hair, and coaxed the chestnut mane to flow over the edge, then laid the towel underneath the dusky strands that touched the floor. He tugged the brush from her stiffened grasp, knelt and began to use it on her hair.

He worked through the tangles patiently, with an unbroken rhythmic gentleness, stroking the dust and the tiny shards of glass out of the silken mass. The act of brushing her hair became an incredible intimacy. He burnished her hair to a lustrous shine, Aladdin polishing his magic lamp.

She endured the sensuous ordeal, feeling the pervading languorous delight as a penance, and when at last she could no longer stand his silence her dark eyes flew open. She looked at his upside-down, intent face and said starkly, 'You are a stranger to me.'

He stopped brushing, an instant freeze, his eyes undertaking a severe dilation. 'Am I?'

'Who are you? I don't know who you are.' It was a very quiet, almost timid whisper.

Adam put aside the brush, for he had rid her hair of the glass splinters long ago. He rolled the towel away, rose up on his knees and cupped her face with both hands, the tips of his forefingers meeting at the point of her chin. He bent over her, his grey eyes ruthlessly probing, and he said in a wise and guttural growl, 'You know me better than you believe. You just won't let yourself see it.'

Her mouth trembled. She felt poised on the edge of a precipice encompassing a huge discovery.

'Think,' he told her. He sounded almost as if he was eager for her to know. Her eyes clung to his and she thought.

Back to the first night they had met, when the Iceman had cracked. 'Yvonne, I'm sorry,' he had said. 'We went too far. I didn't mean to hurt you like that; I didn't know——'

To the second time. 'Yvonne, this needn't be an ordeal. I will challenge you. I can't help it. But I won't push you beyond your limits.'

The third time, his question asked in pain. 'Why do you do it to yourself?'

'Your technique is flawless...I hate it...you're not *giving* anything...'

'I will not suck your soul dry.'

'If you would trust me that far, I would bring you back to yourself. Every time, Yvonne.'

And what she had been fighting and denying from the moment she had met him exploded inside her. Her eyes went wide. She gasped harshly, and would have surged from her supine position on the bed had he not tightened his hard hands around her head and held her prisoner.

His expression had sharpened in predatory triumph at the intense reactive change in hers. He leaned over her unsteady mouth and held his lips just over hers, and did not kiss her. His clean male scent was invasive, inescapable.

'Now do you see?' he said against her lips, in offering and demand.

'No,' she moaned, her legs writhing on the bed as she stared at the hammering pulse underneath the strong bone of his jaw.

'I want you,' he breathed into her mouth. 'I've wanted you since the moment I saw you. I ache at night from thinking about you. I'm hard and dry and nothing and no one else brings me relief. I'm obsessed with the thought of taking you.'

'Stop it!' she cried her panic.

'No.' He said the quiet, inexorable word—a promise, a curse. His hands were shaking now against the curve of her skull, each stiffened digit biting into her overburdened brain. 'You asked for it. You had to ask. It's time you heard the entire truth.'

'I won't listen to you!' She didn't know what she said. She would have recalled the words had she known.

He closed his eyes, his breath a tiny expellation; it was another hurt she had caused him. 'You'll listen,' he said, then grimly, 'By God you will. You deserve to hear it and take responsibility at last for what you've done to yourself. I never wanted you for this film. I hadn't even considered you as a possibility—everybody knew that you had retired. Your father concocted the whole crazy scheme. He always knew he had his part; I'd promised it to him from the very beginning.'

'What?' she shrieked, cried, screamed.

He was blowing her to pieces with methodical precision.

'Then you showed up at your parents' party,' he purred in his primeval growl. 'And you were like nothing I had ever seen before. What you did to me—I was reeling from it. Yes, I grabbed at you, and used every clue you gave away to keep you in Los Angeles. I couldn't believe you were vegetating your life away; I couldn't stand the thought of you disappearing again. You had hidden yourself away in a cave and covered the entrance with a bramble bush, and you weren't ever going to come out. What a wasteland you were.'

Tears sprang into her anguished eyes and spilled over on to his wrists. She sobbed, 'None of it was true?'

'Oh, Yvonne,' he sighed, evocatively, impatiently, and he laid his auburn head on her shaking shoulder. 'All of it was true. Every bit. It just wasn't the understanding you thought it to be. Can you grasp that?'

She was crying, her body labouring with it, her face turned into his warm neck. 'Why did my father do it?'

'He did it because he loves you,' said Adam raggedly. 'He explained it to me at the party after you and I had our argument. And I had already seen your strength, and I recognised in you the possibility of a better Hannah than I had ever before conceived. In one fell swoop I was given the unique actress I was looking for, and a means with which to keep her, and I used it ruthlessly.'

'You're telling me now, after everything that's happened, after everything we've done to each other? I don't understand anything any more!'

'You asked me who I am,' he whispered. He let her go suddenly and surged to his feet, and she sprang into a crouching position on the dishevelled bed and wrapped her tight-clasped arms around her middle and wanted nothing more than for him to hold her prisoner still. He shouted, 'Who am I, Yvonne?'

She whirled, grabbed a pillow and flung it at his rigid figure as hard as she could, crying, 'Don't you shout at me!'

He put his splayed hands on the edge of the bed and leaned on them, his loose shirt gaping open, those broad shoulder muscles bunching massively, and thrust his angry face into hers. 'Don't you tell me what to do,' he growled dangerously. 'Who am I, Yvonne?'

She wiped the back of one hand across her streaked face and breathed hard, her puzzled, devastated eyes searching his rapidly. She was trying desperately to quiet the emotional upheaval inside her, to regain a measure of control, to stop her own wild reaction to what he was doing to her. What was he trying to say to her now?

She gave him what she thought he was looking for, in the form of a question. 'You're not the person I thought you were?'

He closed his eyes slowly and bowed his head, and said with extreme gritty patience, 'Well, I don't know that, do I? I don't know how you saw me—all I can do is guess.'

Sudden comprehension. She was frozen with it, and then she twisted with an abruptness that made the bed rock, and reached with both hands to cup his downbent face and tilt it up to her.

She said with amazement into his grey eyes, 'I thought you were a cold manipulator. I thought you were distant, and superior, and I wondered if you could possibly have any human warmth of feeling at all.'

His gaze darkened into smoky pewter. He said bitterly, 'Iceman Ruarke?'

'Oh, God,' she sighed, and stroked his face. And she had wondered if he could feel pain. 'Of course you'd know about the nickname. You said you read everything.'

He raised a rueful eyebrow. 'I did manipulate you.'

'Well,' she said drily, 'I think I have my own fair share of that personality trait. That's how I got rid of my three nannies, after all.'

Laughter exploded convulsively out from him then, and he turned his face into one of her hands. His skin was so warm, the curve of his mouth such an exquisite pleasure. 'That doesn't mean I forgive you,' she said slowly, as she watched him. 'It just means that I understand you.'

'Better than you thought.' His mouth moved in her sensitive palm and raised the tiny, feathery hairs at the nape of her neck.

Her agreement was shaky. 'Better than I thought. Adam, why did you tell me?'

He reared back from her upraised arms with a violence that made her heart leap in her chest, and he turned away, tilted back his head, rubbed the back of his neck with long fingers.

'Because I got tired,' he told her flatly. 'I got tired of working long hours, and fighting with you every available moment. I got tired of watching you react in all your misunderstandings, tired of maintaining everything and still trying to keep my cool. This has never happened to me before. My concentration is shot to hell.'

Would she ever cease to be amazed by him? The frailties and flaws she had once hoped in desperation to uncover in the winter king he now gave to her with open hands; and contempt had absolutely no part in her reaction to it; and she wasn't about to walk away.

She said gently, 'You've hidden it beautifully. I'm sure no one else knows.'

'You must be joking,' he said with a short bark of a laugh. 'The whole damned lot of them know.'

'No,' she insisted, crawling off the bed and straightening her dishevelled robe into more decency. She walked up behind him and laid a hand on his shoulder, his body heat burning through the thin barrier of his shirt. 'They see us fighting. They see attraction and conflict. But you've still maintained the quality of your work. I've never respected another director the way I respect you. You make me want to work again after two years of drifting in a self-imposed vacuum. You make me want to act better than I ever have before. I'm scared to death of some of the scenes coming up, but I'm also exhilarated.'

He turned his head to one side to listen to her. She never even realised what she had given away in that little speech. She was too busy noticing other things. She saw the hard edge of his cheekbone, the way his auburn hair curled over his shirt collar, could sense the inward curve of his ribs from those wide shoulders to the slim, angled hips, the tight, lean power of his buttocks, the long legs planted well apart.

'I believe I've had an easy time of it for too long,' he remarked in an absent, musing tone, as he rubbed his eyes with thumb and forefinger. 'Maybe I've become complacent.'

She snorted in derision and looked at her hand flattened against the strong, large bone of his shoulder-blade. 'You don't know how to become complacent.'

'You think not?' he replied quietly. 'Don't you recognise the element of truth in your own arguments, and in the nickname the Press gave me? The cold, distant Iceman. I've imitated life too much, I think. The celluloid representation of it has kept me totally absorbed for years, and now I find I'm ravenous to experience the real thing for myself. Do you know, one of the things that blew me away about you was such a stupid little thing you said that first night.'

'What?' she asked, feeling his shoulder muscles move under her hand, a sinuous rippling contraction.

He shifted, and turned around to her in a leisurely fashion, a great sultry beast come to bay. 'You said "fair warning".' Adam smiled, and the look in his beautiful, silver-shot eyes was predatory. 'You were so furious with what you thought I'd done to you, and you still gave me every chance to escape before you pounced. I found the idea—terribly enticing.'

She didn't understand him in this mood. Her eyes grew huge, and she did not know she backed away from him until the back of her knees hit the edge of the bed. 'I only thought to scare you away,' she whispered.

'Oh, dear. I took the message wrong and didn't run,' he murmured mockingly, advancing upon her step by slow, deliberate, prowling step. 'You see, I rather fancied the idea of you leaping on me. It's dictated the course of my actions ever since.'

She panted, her eyes wild and hunted. He hunted her, had hunted her forever, it seemed, unrelentingly, chasing through her thoughts and dreams and every waking moment. 'I—I don't think——' she stammered.

He overrode her ruthlessly. 'Well, I want you to think. I want the knowledge to pound in your blood like a fever. Do you know the real reason why I've told you the truth tonight? You gave me fair warning, and turn-about is fair play. I don't want you reacting any more to the shadows of your own imagination, or to some erroneous concept. Your eyes are going to be wide open to reality and the consequences, and you're going to see me for who I am and know what I've really done to you, down to the very last human mistake.'

'Adam, for God's sake,' she groaned, and his hands whipped out to capture her shoulders.

He yanked her to his naked chest, his fiery head bent down to hers in heated ferocity. She didn't know where to look, and her huge, awestruck eyes ran from his primeval gaze, his mouth, oh, God, his taut, sexy, elegant mouth.

He took a languid fistful of her hair and deliberately positioned her reeling head as his lips parted and he breathed in deeply.

Then his eyes blazed his eloquent intent just one instant before his head drove down on her.

She twisted underneath his invasive kiss, a slow, molten writhe at his unbearable build-up of suspense and the subsequent eroticism of fulfilment. The silken power of his wide chest was a sensory trap for her splayed, weakened fingers.

Perhaps she'd meant to push him away; she'd never know, could never consider the issue, for as her hands connected with his burning, naked skin her whole stunned body reacted. She arced, and her hands slipped all the way around his thudding torso, and her lips twisted under his almost as if she was anguished, as if she was starving, and the moan she gave up to his mouth was a heady liqueur he drank in with greed.

Eyes closed, his throat muscles working, he plunged into her as deeply as he could, passionately, shakingly, in an attempt to assuage the sensual hunger he had endured for so many weeks. The power and force of his passionate need sent them toppling back on to the bed.

Yvonne gasped at the impact but couldn't seem to breathe. Her eyes were open all right, but they weren't functioning. An empty, whirling cloud had taken possession of her body, and the ache of it was only heightened by the hard, pressing weight of his body bearing her into the mattress.

Then he brushed aside her light cotton robe and curled a long hand around the creamy fullness of one breast, running a callused, abrasive thumb over the distended nipple, and the cloud in her became a howling tornado of need.

Adam jerked away from her mouth, reared back his head. The withdrawal contorted his face, hunched his shoulders, distended the tendons at the sides of his neck. His pulse thudded into her, great heavy, clanging strokes of it.

'Oh, God, this is torture,' he groaned hoarsely as she lay spread beneath him, her massive eyes blank with the inexplicable turn of events and her own overwhelming desire. 'I could do it. I could take you right now. I'm so obsessed with the thought of taking you because I won't allow it.'

She twisted underneath him in crazed surprise, and the movement of her body was almost enough to send him over the edge. He shot off her and stumbled back, and connected with the wall behind him, and collapsed into a sitting position on the floor.

She jack-knifed upright and stared at him. He was an astounding sight, his face clenched and beaded with the sweat of his arousal, his wide chest and tight, flat stomach flushed, his long legs splayed, his hooded gaze slumbrous with sexuality.

Adam said, 'Are your eyes wide open now? Do you see me? Are we beginning to understand each other at last?'

He looked drunk; she felt punched. She shrieked at him, 'What do you do to me?'

'That's the beauty of it,' he said. His speech was drowsy and slurred. 'I'll do absolutely nothing to you. That's the secret. If I take you, I will lose you, because you run from the taking every time. Pay attention, darling. If you want me, you'll have to come to me. No victim and perpetrator, no hit-and-run, no trap and no escape. You'll come to me, and you'll touch me, and you'll give of your own volition, or you'll get nothing at all.'

Her mouth opened and closed soundlessly. She really did not know what to think; she couldn't remember how to think at all.

'You're insane.' It was meant as a scream, and came out as a whimper.

He groaned an unsteady laugh and struggled to his feet. It looked like a mammoth effort. 'I know,' he whispered. 'I'm going crazy with waiting, going out of my mind with holding myself in check. It'll probably unman me, but that's how we're going to play it. Don't take too long in making up your mind, will you? The suspense is killing me.'

He was leaving her. He was walking to the door and leaving her aching. The sexual frustration nearly sent her out of her head; she watched his departure and felt as if he was ripping her heart out of her chest with every stride.

'It'll be a cold day in hell before I come to you,' her demon pride snarled, without her approval.

'A cold day in hell could very well be a relief. Beats the thought of a cold shower, at any rate,' he threw over one shoulder with great feeling, then he paused to clench the edge of the door with one whitened hand. He looked back and smiled at her. 'Welcome back to the human race, Yvonne.'

CHAPTER SEVEN

THE next day.

Yvonne hadn't slept. Adam appeared to be just fine.

Fortunately the slight shadows under her eyes enhanced the 'betrayal' scene that was scheduled to be shot that day, where Hannah was to discover her husband in the arms of her sister. She worked like a plough-horse the entire long, hot day, and avoided speaking to anyone if she could help it, aside from saying her lines on cue. Most especially she was not speaking to her father. He didn't, however, get the message very clearly, for he wasn't in any of the scenes and had driven to Phoenix for most of the day.

The day after that.

She looked at food with revulsion. Jerry summoned up his courage and sought her out. He was only concerned about the depth of anger Adam had shown over their little escapade. She nearly bit his head off.

Then she apologised very nicely indeed; after all, what had come after, what hadn't come after—none of it had been his fault. She left the man somewhat puzzled but relieved, then stalked off to have a blazing row with Christopher.

Her father was having none of it. He was patient, and reasonable, and reasonably contrite, and loving, and worried that she could ever forgive him for employing such a deception with the best of intentions. When

Yvonne finally left him, she was wild-eyed with frustration.

The third day.

Adam was everywhere she looked. Strolling past, on his way from here to there. Standing outside, hands on his lean hips, wide shoulders at a negligent angle as he squinted in the intense white sunshine and talked with other cast members, or the cameramen, hearing complaints, taking advice, soothing anybody's ruffled feathers but hers.

Come one, come all, was the winter king's continuous message to the entire complex of people. Come to me, Yvonne, was the message in his eyes whenever he talked to her, ostensibly about mundane things. He was the soul of generosity, he was.

No, I won't, said her haughty dark gaze in stubborn reply.

It was insupportable, unthinkable. Men chased her; she didn't chase them. Men chased and tried to catch her. Come one, come all—she was generous with her rejection, but the one man she most wanted to reject didn't come back.

Inevitably there was a fourth day, and eventually the passing days became a week.

She couldn't believe the fuss she was making, inside her head. Why, she didn't even like sex that much, if her brief and unsuccessful experience years ago had been anything to go by. And why shouldn't it have been? Both she and her only lover had been adults.

The filming went on. Take, take, take. Any taking and she ran away, he had said. She tried to take her ease. She tried to take time off. She tried to take control of her temper, to take comfort in the solitude of her trailer, to take offence. She was sinking in a morass of so much taking that it was taking the heart out of her struggle.

Adam snapped at her over some trifling matter, and she blew up in his face. He seemed unsurprised enough, but their witness, Rochelle, was thoroughly disapproving. She looked at Yvonne with pinched nostrils and walked away, and it was a perfectly ridiculous reaction, for she was the injured party—the—the uninjured party, the party that had had absolutely nothing done to her, aside from a little titillation.

Yvonne knuckled her dry eyes, refused to groan, and then said from between her teeth, 'I'm sorry.'

'Don't mention it,' said Adam mildly, and he walked away. On to another trifling matter; there always seemed to be a crushing mountain of them awaiting his attention.

How could she be jealous of that? But she was; she wanted all his attention on her. Just so that she could reject him? Just so that he was fully aware that she was not—taking—advantage of his invitation? She thought that he was probably well enough aware of that fact already.

'You've gone around the bed, Yvonne,' she whispered to herself, and then was overcome with mortification. Oh, my God, she'd meant to say around the bend.

There was something wrong with Adam's logic. There had to be. She looked and looked for it. Some inadequacy, some human mistake, some unforgivable failing.

She considered the issue obsessively, as she sat side by side with her father under the green-speckled shade of the copse of trees by the river. An array of picnic tables had been set in the area that three times a day was converted into a huge dining area. The catering crew were competent in dealing with the communal meals, and nearly everyone took advantage of their quality cooking. The only other option for most of the crew was to drive into town and pay good money for indifferent service; only the cast of five and Adam, of course, had trailers to themselves and the option of cooking in private whenever it suited them.

The option was a moot point for her, as food continued to look like something she shouldn't be putting in her mouth. That evening the meal had been an all-American cook-out: hot dogs, hamburgers, potato salad, garden salad, brownies, celery and carrot sticks. Ugh. The charcoal smell of the cooking meat in the lingering heat had turned her stomach.

Her gaze followed Adam wherever he went. At the moment he was talking to the catering staff, no doubt praising them for their consistent efficiency. He never stopped. While she slowly darkened under the stress of her solitary fight, he burned with incandescent brightness.

'Dad,' she said abruptly, for she only called him Christopher when she was very, very angry with him, and she had abandoned that some days ago. 'Would you say that males are inherently aggressive?'

Her father followed the direction of her gaze and then he immediately looked somewhere else. 'Well, I don't know,' he said, the perfect picture of idle contemplation; he was a talented man. 'I'm no expert or scientist, but, whether the issue is socialisation or hormones, it seems to me that the male half of the species tends to be more aggressive than the female. Evolution and our own inclinations seem to have cast the male into the role of the hunter, the provider. Not that the female doesn't have her own aggressive tendencies, but perhaps

hers centre more around defence. You know, in protection of home and children.'

'Hah!' Yvonne exclaimed triumphantly, seizing with
greed upon her father's theorising for her own ends. 'I
knew it!'

That explained everything very nicely, thank you.
Adam's professed obsession with taking her, as he de-
scribed it so pithily, and his own subsequent withdrawal.
His own continued inaction. She was primed for defence
but found nothing to defend herself from, and why was
that? Because he didn't really want her as badly as he
had thought he did, that was why. He held back and
went on to other things, and the realisation was a knife-
thrust she guided into her hurting breast.

Her father hadn't finished speaking, however. He
continued thoughtfully, 'We'd be a sorry lot, though, if
we were nothing more than a product of evolutionary
instincts and hormones. No, what I believe is that we
can overcome our basic origins, and choose our own
identity. The individual act of will is the strongest, most
transcendent part of us. To look upon something with
our deepest overriding passions, whether it be rage, grief,
hope or love, and yet recognise a greater need or goal,
and to say, "I will do this" or "I will not do that", no
matter what the personal cost, is a triumph of the spirit.
The exercise of the will is the art of humans in the state
of being.'

As he spoke, her clawed hands curled into the hair at
her temples, and, by the time he had finished, all her
frantic attempts at sweeping Adam out of her life by
virtue of his own inadequacies crashed around her ears
in a thunderous rubble. 'Oh, you're no help!' she said

bitterly to her much mystified parent. 'You're no help at all!'

She thrust to her feet and stalked away, went to her trailer and to her bed, not to sleep; not, perchance, to dream.

Act of will.

'I'm obsessed with the thought of taking you.' 'I'm so obsessed with the thought of taking you because I won't allow it.' 'You run from the taking every time.' 'You'll give of your own volition, or you'll get nothing at all.'

'I could do it. I could take you right now.'

'I want her naked.'

Oh, God, was he going to haunt her for the rest of her waking days? The bond between them had thickened in strength. It pulled on her soul, an unceasing, unendurable call of a siren. She dug in her heels mulishly; she cut off her own nose to spite her face. She was snarled by her own idiotic pride and desire.

Her sensitivity to him had heightened to such an extent that she probably could tell at any given moment where he was, and what he was doing. She contemplated that thought darkly in the cool pre-dawn hours as she cradled a cup of coffee in her hands and sat in a curl on her settee. In a few minutes she would have to leave her trailer and embark upon another long day.

There was a quiet knock upon her door. She never heard it.

She was drowning in the thought of Adam's hair, how it fell upon the hard bone of his brow, how it layered on to his collar, how the sunshine lit the auburn colour with a deep red fire.

Adam opened the door, stuck his head inside and said, 'Yvonne?'

She jumped and squawked, and hot coffee spilled all over her hands and soaked into her dressing-gown. She glared at him and snapped, 'What do you want?'

Poor choice of words. He didn't rise to it, however, and entered the trailer with a serious expression. Absentmindedly he went to the nearby counter that separated the kitchenette from the tiny living space and yanked off a few paper towels from the roll propped by the sink, handing them to her.

'I need to talk to you,' he said. He was coiled into a waiting posture, leaning against the counter as she mopped her sodden front in furious swipes. 'There's been a change in the schedule.'

'What happens today?' she grumbled, not looking at him.

'I've moved up the death scene between Hannah and her father,' he said.

She froze.

Then she moved, her face changing swiftly as her body twisted in protest, and she groaned, 'No, you can't do that—it wasn't supposed to happen for days and days yet——'

'We shoot it today,' he told her very quietly. The expression in his grey eyes as he watched her was dark and troubled.

'But why?' she cried. She looked at him pleadingly. 'Adam, it's too unexpected. I'm not ready for it.'

He breathed deeply, harsh marks scoring twin lines from the flaring curve of nostrils to the tight discipline of his mouth. 'You're ready. You know the lines,' he replied flatly. 'I was looking at the rushes from the other day, and you appear to have lost a few pounds. While I'm concerned about the weight loss, it won't matter in this scene, and then you won't have it hanging over your head. We'll get it over and done with; by the end of the day you won't have to worry about it again.'

He was concerned about weight loss? She looked down at her own body as if it were a stranger's. Her eyes were blank; she hadn't even noticed that she'd lost any weight. 'I'll eat,' she said urgently. 'I'll gain it back. It'll be all right; you don't have to rearrange things.'

His head bowed in weariness, and then he strode over, took her by the arms and lifted her to her feet. He said into her frightened face with harsh ruthlessness, 'Everybody knows the new plan, and you can't change it back. We shoot the scene today. Now I'll tell you what you're going to do, and I want you to follow it step by step. Are you listening?'

She nodded with a dry swallow, her huge eyes clinging to his.

He said gently, 'In a few minutes you're going to go to Christopher. I've already talked to him about it. You're going to sit with him in Make-up, and gossip about all sorts of real-life things. You'll watch his appearance change, and then you're going to do the scene, and you'll go back with him to Make-up and watch it all come off again. I want you to see the illusion for what it really is. Hannah's father dies, but yours will come back to you. Do you understand?'

Her chest was constricted. She understood. He had talked her through meticulously, methodically, and the careful attention to every single detail spoke of immense compassion. She whispered, 'Yes. Thank you.'

He cupped the side of her face and stroked her skin. 'I'm sorry I can't make it any easier on you. We'll take our time, there's no rush or panic, and what happens will happen. If we can't get the scene right today, we won't get it at all. We'll rewrite around it.'

Her sleek eyebrows pulled together. She said slowly, searching his expression, bemused, 'But that will destroy the integrity of the story. His death is integral to the plot.'

He sighed heavily, and whether it was from impatience or remorse she couldn't tell. 'I don't really care. The story's not worth it, not if it costs too much. Are you all right with the change now?'

She wasn't at all sure that she was, but the scene would have to be done sooner or later; as he said, it was best done sooner. She gave him the reassurance he asked for. 'Yes, I'll be fine. Don't worry.'

He gave her an odd look, and shook his head. 'I'll see you both on the set, then,' he said abruptly, and left.

Christopher was waiting for her. He held her hand as the make-up artist painted his face, and the gaunt, haggard apparition he became was a gay and twinkling clown. She laughed at him heartily, knowing fully well what he was doing for her sake, and loved him more than she ever had before because of it.

Then they went to the house, and she hung back as he disappeared into Hannah's father's bedroom with Adam. She waited, her heart pounding as she listened to the murmur of the two men's voices, until Adam came out again.

He smiled at her, and said easily, 'That's it, then. The camera's going to start rolling as soon as you walk into the room. We're not going to cut, but don't let that worry you. Just take your time, break out of character if you have to, and get it over with.'

They weren't going to cut? What an extravagant waste of expensive film; mistakes and mischievous pranks sprinkled the crew's everyday life, but camera time was sacrosanct. It was an immense gift he offered. She smiled back at him, blindingly, and whispered, 'Thank you.'

'Whenever you're ready,' he murmured, and kissed her forehead, and then he walked back into the room. He would be waiting unobtrusively, out of sight behind the cameraman, but she had to dismiss him from her thoughts.

Yvonne was staggered by the trust, by the consideration, by the sheer love and respect everyone gave to her. She couldn't fail them; she couldn't let that happen; this meant too much. It went far beyond the boundaries of movie-making and an imitation of life. It had absolutely nothing to do with either the pursuance or abandonment of a career.

She closed her eyes and centred herself. She had no idea if she could act the scene. She was a pauper in the face of such rich human experience, and, since she had nothing else she could give them in return, she would give them Hannah.

She walked to the doorway. The sight of the still, pale figure in the bed slammed into her; the echo of the blow halted her and shook across her face.

'Dad?' she asked, a fragile and fearful thread of sound. 'Daddy?'

The figure didn't move, didn't breathe. The silence of the room was vast. She couldn't approach him, and skirted around the edge of the room, her eyes swallowing up the rest of her face, eloquent, despairing, hor-

rified eyes. She was failing; this was too much for her.
Her lips trembled, and then her whole body followed in
terrified concert.

'I can't do this,' she whispered, holding on to the wall.
'I don't know what it means. Oh, God, please sit up.'

And the figure didn't move. It was unbearable. She
couldn't bear it. She flung herself across the room and
across her father, her hands clenched into the sheets
covering his chest and her head bowed over them, the
classic posture of a woman in the terrible discovery of
grief. She sobbed from the bottom of her soul, 'I love
you, Daddy.'

The lines she spoke were more than flawless. The lines
came from her brand new. Adam leaned his head against
the wall and said rawly to the cameraman, 'Stop filming.'

The man looked over his shoulder. He had been totally
absorbed in the pathos of the scene. 'What?' he whispered incredulously. 'But this is fantastic——'

'Stop filming, goddammit!' The powerful roar shattered the atmosphere. Yvonne's overflowing eyes blinked
several times in rapid succession, and Christopher shot
to a sitting position and wrapped his arms around her.
Then the pair, father and daughter alike, turned as one
to stare at their director in puzzlement and enquiry.

Adam looked at them both, at the dark eyes so much
alike and yet so different. He was white, the incan-
descence bleached out of him. A true actor became his
part, not merely played it. Where were his limits?

'You're finished for the day,' he told them through
stiffened lips. 'We'll use whatever we've got.'

They had barely started. She protested, amazed, 'But
Hannah's got more lines to say.'

'*No more, Yvonne,*' he said, with one fist upraised, and he nearly knocked the cameraman over as he stalked out of the room.

Yvonne looked up at Christopher, her expression full of bewilderment. 'What did I do wrong?'

'Nothing, darling,' soothed her father, who pressed her chestnut head to his chest and took advantage of the fact to wipe his face surreptitiously. 'You did beautifully.'

But she didn't believe him. She was worried and disappointed; Adam had told her once that she gave nothing to her performance, and then, when she had tried to give so much, he cut her short. She always seemed to be floundering in the land of confusion where he was concerned, never managing to grasp the relevant point.

'He's just tired, that's all,' she decided out loud, and nodded. 'He's been working too hard. That's it. Everybody else has a day off here and there but, as director, Adam never gets a break. It must be a terrible strain. I really don't know how he does it.'

The lack of response to her words finally brought her mumbling to a halt, and she glanced around for confirmation. Both the cameraman and her father were looking at her as if she'd lost her mind.

Her shoulders slumped. Who was she trying to fool? Herself, that was who. Only and always herself.

Adam had left the site. No one knew where he'd gone, just that he had decided that everyone was going to take the rest of the day off, and he'd got into his car and driven away. The cat was away and the mice got down to some serious play. A softball game was set up, a party planned for the evening, beer bought.

Everybody else thoroughly enjoyed the brief hiatus. Yvonne found the whole thing very wearying. She went to bed early, and made the resolution between the midnight hours and morning that she would try even harder the next day to give Adam what he wanted, to perform to the utmost of her capabilities, to live up to his expectations. She couldn't bear to look into his grey eyes and see disappointment.

She thought it would be easy the next day, a piece of cake. She'd hardly have to do any acting at all, for her reactions were much in keeping with Hannah's distaste when her husband tried to make love with her.

She and Richard had carefully plotted out the whole thing. Actually, knowing Richard's true lightheartedness, it was difficult to keep a straight face during the rehearsals, and they'd broken out of character several times to guffaw at one another's clumsiness. The laughter was a defence mechanism for both of them, for his nature was repelled as much as she by his character's actions. He'd handled the preparations with tremendous finesse and unfailing consideration. She was very much impressed with him; there was more substance to the butterfly man than most people suspected.

Prompt as ever the next day, Yvonne settled into her canvas chair outside and idly swung one bare leg while she waited. She'd had a lazy morning drinking coffee and reading the papers, for she wasn't needed until the afternoon. She was in costume, barefoot and wearing a drab, faded cotton dress that buttoned to the waist, and raring to go.

Adam stood some fifteen feet away with his back to her, a rigid, unmoving statue. He'd been that way for the last twenty minutes; sometimes his patience was downright uncanny. He studied the scene, waiting for the afternoon sunshine to enter the barn at just the right angle.

Richard sauntered over to her. Gone was his usual sleek sophistication and a sweaty, brawny farmer had taken his place. She looked him up and down and made a rude noise through her patrician nose. He grinned, unoffended.

He dropped a light hand on to her shoulder. 'OK about it?'

She nodded and rubbed her feet back and forth on the ground to make them even more dirty. 'We'll do it just as we said.'

'That's it,' said Adam suddenly at last. 'Everybody out of the barn except the two cameramen. We shoot in five minutes.'

The crew scrambled. Adam swung about and stalked up to Richard and Yvonne.

She watched him warily. She had never found out where he had gone, or when he had got back. The break had not apparently refreshed him, for his mood was still as black and as volcanic as it had been yesterday. He scared and confused her in the mood he was in, his expression hard-bitten, stress stamping harsh lines in his face, the grey eyes flat and unrevealing as stone. He carried his gracefully proportioned body with dangerous violence.

Adam halted in front of them. He said to the other man, 'I want no nudity. You know what you're supposed to do.'

'Right,' said Richard, so heartily cheerful that she winced.

Adam's shotgun eyes were fierce on the other man. He groaned from between his white teeth, 'Treat her with respect, Richard.'

The actor squirmed. Yvonne didn't blame him. Adam looked ready to tear him apart with his bare hands. 'Hell, Adam,' said Richard plaintively. 'Respect her? She frightens the daylight out of me in real life.'

She shot out one stiffened fist and punched him in the leg, and Richard rolled his eyes comically and groaned.

Adam didn't laugh. He said softly, 'Get in your places.'

How it was supposed to go: Hannah would be in the barn taking care of the animals when her husband came. There would be some uncomfortable dialogue, then he was to grab her and force her down into the hay. Simple enough?

The first take. Richard tripped over the short milking-stool.

Adam said, 'Cut. Do it again.'

The second take. Yvonne stubbed her bare toe and hopped in one-legged agony all over the barn.

'Cut. Do it again.'

The third take. One of the milk cows took it into her head to moo a mournful song, and had to be led out of the barn.

The fourth take. Adam's unbroken deadly quiet was beginning to affect everyone. Yvonne found herself quite inexplicably shaking with nerves. They started over, and the dialogue and movements went without a hitch. This time it looked as if they were going to get through the excruciating scene; she found herself actually sighing with relief as Richard successfully threw her into the artfully padded hay and fell on top of her.

Her part was relatively easy. She braced her hands on his shoulders and arched her back away from him, averting her contorted face—towards one camera—in helpless disgust. Almost done now.

Oh, poor Richard. He was one tangled-up puppy. Somehow he had pinned part of her dress underneath one of his big hands that he braced his weight on, and as she arced and he shifted the thin faded cotton ripped from collar to waist.

He froze and they both looked down her front. She wasn't wearing a bra, and her flesh from throat to navel was an unbroken clean line between the exposed swell of her breasts. She had room to think, ruefully, that it could have been worse; at least her nipples were covered.

Richard's eyes shot up to hers in horrified apology. She grimaced at him in good-natured forgiveness—and Adam plucked the actor off her body, threw him against the side of a stall, and pinned him by the throat.

'What the *hell* do you think you're doing?' he snarled hoarsely, his feral eyes molten pools of silver. 'I said no nudity!'

Dear God. Yvonne lay sprawled at their feet and stared up at the two men in severe shock. Richard, big man that he was, dangled in Adam's strangling grip like a child, his mouth hanging open. Adam's body, from the broad shoulders angled over the tight hips to the bulging extension of the long arm spearing towards the other man's suffused neck, was one sweeping, powerful weapon of aggression.

She scrambled to her feet, one hand clutching the torn edges of her dress together, the other hand shooting out to tug at Adam's arm. It felt like trying to bend a bar of iron. 'Adam, stop it!' she yelled sharply into his insane face. 'It was an accident!'

Then came one of the most painful things she'd ever had the misfortune to witness. The slow, hard birth of realisation overcame the blind ferocity in Adam's eyes; the civilised man returned to inhabit the body of the marauding beast, and was sickened with what he found there.

The long hand at Richard's throat loosened, and fell away. He straightened, his face like stone, his eyes like marble rocks, as the other man gasped. He said quietly, 'I'm so sorry, Richard. I don't know what came over me. Are you all right?'

'Quite all right,' the actor gurgled, his eyes askance. 'Don't mention it.'

Adam wiped his face with a shaking hand, his struggle for control awesome in its extremity. 'I think we're through filming for today,' he said in that deadened, polite voice. 'Wrap it up and go to dinner, gentlemen.'

Then he turned and walked into the sunshine that brought his erect, regal figure into pitiless exposure, and he disappeared.

Yvonne stared into the space he had occupied. She was rooted to the ground where she stood. He hadn't even looked at her.

Richard touched her arm with a tentative hand. 'Yvonne, I'm sorry——'

'Oh, don't you start too, you silly man,' she said through numb lips. 'Are you really all right?'

'Oh, sure.' Richard had bounced back like a rubber ball and waved away the little scene with a careless hand and a laugh. 'I mean, that wasn't anything compared to some of the fights we got into three years ago when I was filming a movie in——'

She looked at him, her dark gaze terrible. The actor coughed the rest of the sentence away. 'I don't understand why he did it,' she said blankly. 'I thought we were doing fine until he—lost his temper.'

Richard's eyes sparkled with worldly amusement. He drawled intimately, for her ears alone, 'Perhaps it had something to do with the fact that he couldn't stand the sight of another man touching your delicious body, even in make-believe.'

Yvonne looked as if he had just dumped a ton of bricks on to her head. The actor smiled at her, patted her ashen cheek like an uncle, and strolled off, whistling, to his supper.

She didn't know how long she stood there, blinking at nothing in particular, listening to the airy, dust-mote-filled silence. It must have been forever.

When she finally moved, she started out calmly. She strolled to the dressing trailer, let the costume designer cluck over the ruined dress, and slipped on a terry robe. Then she went to her own trailer. Dinner, she could see from one of her windows, was being served outside. Adam wasn't anywhere to be seen.

Then she began to up-momentum. She quickly showered, dragged on oxfords, a pair of shorts and a T-shirt. By the time she noticed the hay sticking out of her hair, she was frantic, and yanked her hairbrush through the mass with brutal disregard for her appearance or her own scalp. When she exploded out of the door and down the steps, she was going at high speed and gunning for full throttle. Her long legs flashed as she raced across the deserted expanse to Adam's trailer.

She had left it too late to meet him halfway. That she would have had to do the night he had been in her trailer. Please let him be there. Please don't let him be gone.

She had such a long, long way to go.

CHAPTER EIGHT

YVONNE burst into Adam's trailer.

Her entry was unsubtle. The door banged against the outside and then whipped back to slam shut with a force that nearly ripped it from its hinges. She managed to rocket to a halt before her impetus sent her crashing into the opposite wall, and she stood there swaying back and forth on the balls of her feet, trying to recover her equilibrium.

Adam sat at the small dining-table that was littered with computer paper, broad shoulders hunched, his auburn head in his hands. He didn't bother to look up. He bit out harshly, 'Whatever it is, just leave it until morning. I don't want to hear about it.'

Her brow wrinkled in distress. He wasn't supposed to say that. Didn't he listen to everybody? This couldn't wait, she decided as she stared down at her hands, and for lack of anything better to do with them she twisted them together.

'I get all tangled up sometimes, you know?' she said. Her narrow fingers locked together urgently, and unlocked, and reconfigured.

'Yvonne,' said Adam, his voice flat with hostility, 'get out.'

That hurt badly enough to send her pacing.

'It gets snarled, all of it,' she said agitatedly, her head bent. She went into the kitchenette space, turned around, and blundered straight into a cabinet. 'It's just a big

135

snarl. I don't quite know how to get out of it half the time. I fight so hard and come to a standstill, and there's nothing around me but just this——'

She waved her hands in the air. The silence behind her was so intense that for all she knew she was talking to the cabinet. She said to it, conversationally, 'I make myself crazy. I can't imagine why anyone would want to be around me.'

'Oh, for God's sake,' he sighed. The chair scraped across the floor as he rose to his feet.

She whirled around at the sound and stared at his harsh, downbent expression, and her own was blanched with terror and pleading. Her whisper came out strangled, 'The first time I ever—well, you know—I couldn't help thinking that it was some huge, awful mistake. I was hopeless at it, I didn't get the point, I just felt—weighed down and thought that if this is what it takes to propagate the human race it's a wonder our species didn't die out ages ago....'

His head had lifted. His gaze fixed on her as she rambled almost into incoherence. Then she had a thought for how utterly ridiculous she sounded and stumbled to a halt, and her already gibbering brain went into a deep freeze as she watched a dark colour wash over his hard cheekbones, and his grey eyes take fire.

'Yvonne?' Her name, on his lips, was a question.

She said shudderingly, 'Oh, help.'

One fierce stride took him to the edge of the counter. He was opening up his arms, and she shot into their welcome like an arrow to the gold.

The impact of chest upon chest could have been a little easier. She wasn't sure whether he staggered, or she had, or maybe the earth had moved just a little...

He crushed her to him and buried his face into her chestnut hair. No, the earth hasn't moved, you idiot, she told herself. *She* was moving, everywhere, in violent, involuntary, teeth-chattering shivers. She felt stricken with pneumonia, racked with chills, raging with fever, and was dead certain she would sustain structural damage.

She felt the deep, hard breath he dragged into his lungs, and then he was quiet, his body held in perfect control. He brought up one hand to cup the back of her head, under the fall her hair, and he pressed her face into the side of his neck.

'Shh,' he whispered, soothing her shivering back with long calm strokes of his other hand. 'Slow down, baby. Quiet down.'

She groaned, appalled, overcome, reduced. 'I c-can't stop—I can't h-help it——'

'It's all right,' he murmured. He spread his long legs apart and rocked her a little. 'You're here now. It's OK.'

Was it? Was it OK? Her hands were clenched in the shirt material that covered the small of his back as she considered. It didn't feel OK to her. It felt so powerful and mind-destroying that she thought she might break apart into tiny pieces flinging outwards from a centrifugal force.

'Maybe this isn't a good idea,' she whispered into his neck, burrowing into him like a small animal desperate for cover. 'I'm not exactly known for them. I should have come earlier or not at all. I don't know why I waited so long; I'm always fighting——'

His hard, large torso moved; the tight strength of his hands on her felt as though he would break through her bones. 'Do you regret it already?' he gritted harshly.

'I don't know!' she cried with the force of all the confusion inside her.

The hand cupping the delicate curve of her skull twisted into her hair, and he yanked her head back to glare into her wide eyes. He growled, 'You came because you wanted to. You're here because you want to be here. Don't you dare try to tell yourself anything different.'

'Well, yes and no,' she said weakly. She wasn't at all sure she should be saying such things to him. It was too graceless, too exposing, and yet the words flooded from her mouth ungovernably; they were an explanation and a barrier to the consequences of her own actions, the consequences she didn't want to think about. 'I didn't want to want it. That's the point. It's a worry and a complication.'

'A—worry and a complication,' he echoed queerly, his grey eyes blackened with such a severe onslaught of internal fury that she flinched in miserable reaction and half expected him to strike at her. Then, amazingly, he hunched his shoulders and hugged her to him with an eloquence of expression so outside the range of her expectations that she shuddered anew and moaned, a short, tiny betrayal of vulnerability. She heard herself and was shocked, and clamped her throat muscles into abrupt silence.

'Dear lord,' he was saying, savagely, absently to himself. 'I don't think I've actually hated anyone before. I've never wanted to hurt anyone the way I want to hurt the man who did this to you. A worry and a complication; my God, you have absolutely no idea why you came here tonight, do you? You don't even know what you've been fighting. No wonder it took you so long, no wonder you're in such a state. I thought you were teasing me. I've wanted to strangle you countless times this last week, and ended up taking it out on everyone else instead, because I was afraid that if I blew up at you I really wouldn't be able to remember when to stop.'

'I felt as if I couldn't seem to do anything right,' she whispered. One corner of her brain said, Stop confessing so much, stupid, but still she couldn't help herself. Still the need for reassurance came shining out of her words. Her pride had got her into so much trouble that she'd left it at the door. 'The death scene; today with Richard. I've tried so hard to get it right, and I don't know what else to do.'

His sigh was a heavy reply, gusting through the feathery hairs at her temple. 'Then I couldn't have made a bigger mess of things had I tried,' he said in grim self-disgust. 'Yvonne, don't argue for once, don't fight what I tell you, just listen to me. Your performance has been— exemplary. You've gone from giving nothing to giving more and more every time you get in front of the camera. You're giving so much, it humbles me. For the first time in my career I don't quite know what to do with it all. I've misplaced my objectivity; I'm straining at the edge of a creative crisis. I nearly killed Richard today for what he was doing to you because I misplaced Hannah and her husband, and I forgot that the real man would never be capable of doing to you what Hannah's husband did to her. I don't know how I'm going to look him in the face tomorrow.'

Her mind shot back to what the actor had whispered to her in the barn, and it was the one thing she couldn't bring herself to confess to him, the one thing she suspected he wouldn't be able to hear.

'Richard,' she said instead, darkly and with a covert wisdom, 'laughed at me. He told me war stories of his previous films which far outweighed your loss of temper, and then went whistling off to his supper without a care in the world. If I were you, I wouldn't waste any more time agonising over *his* finer sensibilities; the man just doesn't have any.'

She held her breath, and waited, and nearly sagged with relief at her success when his taut posture relaxed, the powerful muscles shifting fluidly against her torso, and he emitted a dry ghost of a laugh.

'Speaking of suppers,' he murmured, his touch moving to the shell curve of her ear to finger it with a delicacy that made her shudder, 'you should eat something.'

He could think of food at a time like this? She gritted her teeth and growled, 'I'm not hungry.'

He didn't move. Why did she feel as if a thousand-watt jolt of electricity had just coursed through his body?

'No,' he breathed in a sultry croon, 'but you will be.'

She pulled back her head, searched the heated glitter in his eyes, and snapped in warning, 'Don't try to shove anything down my throat. I'll eat when I want to, and not a moment before.'

She must have read the message wrong; she must have misunderstood, for he smiled in slow, ferocious anticipation, and said simply, 'OK. Let's go to bed instead.'

She froze, not quite able to accept the evidence of her own ears, and stared at him, rabbit-like, caught in the twin glare of approaching headlights.

He let her go and strolled languidly over to the door, and locked it. His movements were shattering, deliberate; she was overcome with anxiety and disappointment. Whatever she had expected to happen in coming here tonight, this definitely wasn't any part of it. If anything, from Adam, she had expected more—finesse.

He walked back over to her, and the fulminating expression on her angular face was almost enough to make him smile. He put an arm around her slim shoulders and said quietly, 'Come on, then.'

Well. She had made her choice, hadn't she? She would just have to put up with it. If nothing else came out of it, at least tomorrow she wouldn't be so eaten up with the obsession that had dogged her footsteps for what felt like an eternity now. Still, it *was* a worry and a complication.

She turned, pliant as a doll, and walked with him down the short hall to the darkened bedroom.

Adam led her straight to the bed without bothering to turn on the light. The only illumination was diffuse, silvery, the far-away weakened overspill from the light still shining in the kitchenette. She turned her huge, overwrought eyes to his shadowy figure. She heard everything—the whispery brush of his jeans as he walked, the slight, almost negligible friction of their shoes on the carpet.

Now what? She took the bottom edge of her T-shirt in shaking hands and would have lifted it over her head, but he forestalled her. 'Don't undress,' he murmured. 'Just lie down on the bed with me.'

What was this? He kicked off his shoes; she followed suit. Then he lay down on the bed, on his back and stretching out his long length with a weary sigh, and his head turned on the pillow towards her. She stared at the shadowy glimmer of his eyes as he held open his arms.

She was too weak to remain upright. She went down to him like wax. She was too rigid to relax. She tried to force her frozen muscles into compliance and broke into another involuntary rash of trembling.

He guided her untidy head to rest on his shoulder. She curved her body to fit to the length of his. She struggled to find something to say, found nothing but a roaring emptiness inside her head, and started to breathe unevenly.

He rested the side of his cheek against her forehead, his arms wrapped firmly and without urgency around her quaking body, one hand splayed along the long line of the side of her neck. His little finger rested on her collarbone, the forefinger touching her ear, the thumb rubbing slowly across the soft skin beside her bewildered mouth. He was so big; he could snap her with one careless flick of the wrist.

'Just relax, baby,' he murmured peaceably. 'You're not going anywhere.'

She lay beside him, her mind in a rabid, compulsive whirl.

Long, silent moments ticked by, and he did nothing to her. He was a tired and overworked man, and by the very stillness of his posture she suspected he had probably gone to sleep.

As first nights went, it was certainly an unusual one. She wondered if she was disappointed really, and thought that probably she was, but the feeling was overshadowed with a sense of relief. So much for overwhelming passion; so much for her over-active imagination.

His shoulder was a broad, warm, comfortable pillow. She snuggled into it, rubbing her cheek against his fragrant shirt, and listened to the steady, unhurried beat of his heart. Gradually she adjusted to his large presence; gradually her tense, unstable limbs quietened and relaxed.

After a long time, she shifted to get into a more comfortable position, moving with careful stealth for fear of waking him. She fitted herself more snugly around the contours of his body. One of her legs was flush down the side of his, his body heat filtering through the material of his jeans and keeping her comfortably warm. The other leg she bent at the knee and hitched up over him, the length of her inner thigh lying across his hips. Her arm was flung across his wide chest, and she rested her narrow fingers in the hollow of his neck.

He didn't move at all. He hardly seemed to be breathing. Why, this had actually evolved into quite a delightful experience, succumbing to the sensuality of sharing his bed, the animal comfort of his body, the soft and gentle permeation of co-existing side by side with him. She was languid, drugged with the evidence of him, suffused with a heaviness that drooped her eyelids.

Maybe she was too heavy, she thought sleepily. Maybe being draped all over him like a wet dishrag was uncomfortable for him. She shifted as if to pull away, and the weight of her thigh rubbed against his crotch.

He groaned and went rigid. 'Don't move.'

She froze in surprise. He wasn't asleep? The trailer was air-conditioned but the skin of his neck underneath her fingers broke into a sweat.

'I thought I might be too heavy for you,' she whispered.

'No,' he grunted briefly, but he sounded as if he was in agony. 'You're perfect, but just don't wiggle any more, OK?'

'OK,' she murmured. She loved the feel of his hand lying along her face and tilted her jaw under the broad width of his palm. God, his heat had increased until he felt as if he was burning up.

She had never been held in such a way. She had never been cuddled with such a quality of feeling, his very comportment a statement of intimate recognition, the posture of his body an indication of intense awareness of every line and hollow of her own body, and a depth of knowledge for the weight distribution of her muscles. He was perfectly disposed, perfectly arranged for her physical comfort. It made her feel—cherished.

Her breathing was deep and even, her lips parted slightly. She started to drift.

Then he lifted his hand and stroked her face. His touch was light, gentle, beautiful.

His fingers were shaking.

She was overcome with drowsy astonishment, and turned to kiss them into steadiness. He dragged the callused tips over the lush velvet of her lips, and then with quite exquisite care insinuated his forefinger into her mouth. She murmured a wordless enquiry, her lips parting as naturally as the petals of a flower unfurling, her strengthless head lying back along his arm.

His finger rubbed along the moist interior of her lower lip. The pleasure of it was incredible. It did the strangest things to her, all over her body. The tip of her tongue touched him, delicately, involuntarily. His finger probed deeper, stroked the length of her tongue, back and forth, rubbed along the hard ridges of her teeth.

Her breathing started to become a ragged struggle. She was a boneless mass of sensation, while he had become even more rigid than ever, his arm around her back crushing her against the side of his body, his hard cheekbone digging into her forehead. His pulsebeat had started a jack-hammering in her ear; his lips were parted in great audible gasps as he moved his finger in her mouth.

She loved it, she really did, but it was making her crazy. She wanted his finger to continue its torturous caress, but she found she wanted his mouth on hers more. She found she wanted his mouth more and more. Instinct made her lips clamp around the length of his finger and she sucked him hard and quick, and then thrust him out of her mouth.

He groaned aloud, and erupted like a spewing volcano.

Suddenly she was flat on her back, and he had heaved over her. He held himself planted on his hands and knees on either side of her body, his heated gaze ravishing the curves and lines of her face. His taut expression was primeval.

Then his head swooped down. Just his head. Just his lips, fastening hotly over hers and slanting open, and his tongue piercing her to the quick, just what she wanted.

Her head raised off the pillow as she kissed him back. Her whole torso curved to meet the fierce demand; she raised herself up on her elbows, hands clenched into the bedspread. She was straining, trying to pierce herself even further, wanting to impale herself on the source of her agony.

He pulled away from her, and she fell back on the pillow and cried, 'Don't——'

Don't go, don't stop.

His face was anguished. He squeezed his eyes shut and gritted his teeth, and after a moment he was able

to look at her; the eye contact was searing. He laid a
hand around the curve of her throat, and his ravening
gaze shot down the length of her reclining body.

'Yvonne,' he whispered hoarsely, fingering the collar
of her top, 'take off your T-shirt.'

'What?' She hardly knew what he was saying to her.
She raised her hands and tried to entice his body down
to hers. Then she raised herself up, and slowly pulled
the top over her head.

He clenched his fists into the material of the bedspread on either side of her head, staring down at her.
She shook all over, shocked by the erotic savagery in his
gaze; he growled deep in his chest, 'Oh, God, your
breasts are so lovely. I've waited too long to touch them.
Please, may I?'

The savagery and the pleading; the passion and the
control; the physical and the verbal; the patience and
the desperation. He was fused, undeniable, all things
and all men at once, a coalition and an autocrat.

She lay displayed to him in all her finery and foibles,
her chestnut hair whirled around her head, the massive
eyes hooded, the expression on her face amazed and
slumbrous, her lips swollen and beautiful, the curve of
her breasts generously rising to precise, upraised peaks.

She would give herself to him, or she would get nothing
at all. She ran her tongue around her dry lips, a victim
to the fever he had perpetrated, hit by the running lava
in her veins, trapped by the escaping passion. 'Please,
Adam,' she whispered unsteadily. 'Please take me.'

His eyes flared up to hers, and his handsome face
shook with the realisation of what she gave to him. And
then came tenderness, a realm of it vast enough to build
an entire kingdom on, to flourish in forever.

And then he came down to her, and he took her with such complex and minute dexterity, with such unrelenting, shuddering, rhythmic force, with such consummate stamina and finality, that when he came to the end of his endurance and shot forth her name in an exultant hawk's cry she arced and flooded with the immensity of completion.

She was entranced. She was entrenched.

They lay together in a naked tangle of trembling limbs, and she had no thought at all for fighting her way out of the bodily snarl.

The taste of his salty sweat was delicious, the brute magnificent, and the indignity of her shredded clothing lay all around them like moulted feathers. Yvonne laughed and licked his damp, heaving shoulder. Adam cocked a rueful eyebrow against the side of her cheek and closed his eyes.

'How am I going to get back to my trailer, in just my shoes?' she whispered into his ear. It was a useless hypothesis. She doubted she could even stand upright, let alone walk.

His arms tightened on her. He growled, 'You're not going anywhere. You're staying right where you are, flat on your back. Oh, damn, we've got to retake the blasted barn scene tomorrow. I want to mark you. I want to mark you all over your thin, luscious skin, to tell the entire world that I put the marks there, to show them that you're mine.'

He had already marked her, in places the camera, or anyone else for that matter, would never see.

'Hush, you fool.' The words were harsh, the way she murmured them an endearment, as she covered his elegant mouth with her fingers, and then replaced them with her lips.

'Fool, she says,' he murmured, caressing the corner of her mouth with intense fascination for its texture and shape. 'Hush, she says. The woman knows how to seduce without putting forth the slightest effort at seduction. She does it by being herself. She does it by *being*, without artifice or flirtation. The woman just is, and is bewildered by it.'

'Adam?' she whispered shakenly.

Adam?

'Go to sleep, Yvonne,' he said, and he dragged the covers over them both, and wrapped his arms around her in an unbreakable, possessive hold.

Where did she go? She wasn't going anywhere. She went nowhere at the speed of light. She closed her eyes, snuggled against him, and fell asleep.

After a dark and dreamless time, her eyes flew wide open. From one moment to the next, she was wide awake, and not quite sure what had awakened her. Then she knew the answer: she was alone in Adam's bed. The crack between the curtains was still black, the illumination was still silvery and indirect, but she had a feeling of time that had passed and was not to be recalled. The bedside clock told her it was four-thirty in the morning.

The door of the trailer opened and closed. Very quietly Adam walked down the hall towards the bedroom. Very quickly Yvonne shut her eyes and pretended to be asleep, then looked at him covertly through her slitted lashes.

He wore only a faded pair of jeans. His hair was so dark as to appear black and lay sleek along the strong contours of his head. Her sensitive nostrils caught the faint fresh scent of soap; he had already showered.

He moved with such care, so as to not wake her. When he reached her side of the bed, he put a small pile of clothes on the floor. He must have gone to her trailer to find something for her to wear. She nearly smiled then, for her entire body was completely, falsely lax and her heart pounded hard and quick with a hunter's thoughts.

The winter king was exquisite prey, hard and muscled and ineffably graceful, from the rippling width of breast muscles to the long, undulating flat stomach, and the heavy bulge of thighs.

He squatted beside her for the longest time, and she nearly lost her control as she felt—felt, as a physical manifestation, his eyes roaming over her sleep-flushed, serene face and the upturned curl of one outflung hand, the only two things that lay uncovered by the tangled sheet. He touched her palm, a light delicacy not designed to awaken, and she had to restrain the dark desire to clamp her fingers over his hand.

Then he left the bedroom. The predator heard him moving languidly around the kitchenette, and rose in panther-like silence, wrapping the sheet, somehow, toga-like around her taut body.

She began to stalk. She paused in the shadow of the hall and watched him. Still he appeared to be unaware of her. Anticipation made her eyes dilate to ravenous, shining pools of blackness, her fine nostrils flare, her mouth go dry.

His coffee was made. He poured himself a cup, then just stood at the counter, his weight on one leg, the other at an indolent angle. One would almost think he was posing that beautiful body in all its male pride and virile strength for her. One would almost—he sighed and rotated his auburn head, and then in a glorious act of unselfconsciousness he put both hands to the small of his back and arced his spine in a great, bone-cracking stretch. It bent back those straight shoulders and widened his sculpted chest, and narrowed the gorgeous abdomen under the curved cage of his ribs where a fine dark arrow of hair shot into the confinement of the faded jeans.

The predator's intent wait was over; her control snapped. She flowed into the kitchenette, a prowling feline driven by hunger, and his damp auburn head turned towards her.

In the winter king's eyes was vast amusement.

He had known the entire time that she was awake, and watching him.

Take me, his gaze said.

She let go of the sheet. It fell to the floor. She was shaking with need when she reached to undo the fastening of his jeans, her ferocious gaze holding his unblinkingly. He positioned his body, leaning that powerful body back against the counter in a display of surrender. Her fingers found the zip and pulled it down. He was already a hardened inferno.

Her thick lashes swept down to hide the sparkle of intent in her eyes as she thought to take her revenge on his subterfuge. As she pulled the jeans down the length of his legs, she followed them to the floor in a slow, graceful fall.

She knelt before him, her naked body curled, and the light in the kitchenette shone on the slender wings of her shoulderblades, the hourglass curve of her tiny waist and flaring hips, the knobs and hollows of her spine a vulnerable submission. She stroked his thighs in a light, chaste caress.

That was how she broke the winter king's controlled surrender. Not in screaming rage or defiance, not in tempestuous explosion, not in indomitable pride, or with straight-backed fire, all those characteristics he saw, and was aroused by, and admired in her. She brought him down with humility.

He groaned and came to his knees, and grabbed her downbent head to drag her up and kiss her searingly, shakingly. He was the victor, as he fell to the floor and yanked her astride him, and held the jutting bowl of her hips above him, and plunged inside her. He was the victor, and that was his downfall.

His entry was a massive fulfilment. Her head flung back as she arced instinctively at the impalement, and cried her trembling desire. His grey eyes were ruthless, incredulous. She took him, she took all of him on a wild ride of no return and the sweetest of violent endings.

The sight of her helpless climax made him spill into her with such force that his face contorted, and his entire body shook as if with ague. Then the slender feminine power that had sustained her flew out of her body like a capricious spirit, and she collapsed atop him in a fragile, strengthless heap.

She shuddered against his thudding chest, her breathing in barely audible moans, the release of intolerable stress. He stroked her compulsively, murmuring something guttural and incoherent.

Her hair covered them both in a glossy velvet blanket. It hid her face, for which she was so grateful, as her mouth bowed and her eyes filled and overspilled. His skin was so wet, he would never notice the added moisture.

Act of will.

She had looked at him with her deepest overriding passions. She had watched him peak, and it was beautiful.

I will not love him, she whispered in her secretive heart of hearts.

CHAPTER NINE

SOMETHING had happened to her.

Inevitably they separated, to prepare to meet the demands of the long, sun-drenched day. Yvonne showered and dressed in the clothes Adam had brought back for her, and went back to her trailer in an absent, weaving meander.

The sense of loss at leaving him, already preoccupied with the mountain of papers on the dining-table, had been strangely intense. She had kissed him on the forehead; he had caressed her cheek with long, hard fingers, then turned back to his work. It was only sensible of him. She quite understood that. Their early morning lovemaking had already made him start later than he had originally intended, a later start to a day that was more pressured than ever, with the make-up work from the previous afternoon on top of the original schedule.

She drifted through her trailer like an abandoned, forlorn ghost who had misplaced the purpose of its haunting. For God's sake, what was she wanting? She'd had a night of passion and fulfilment that quite took her breath away. It had been far more than she could have ever expected, hoped for, feared, longed for, dreamed of. She was sated, heavy-eyed, her nipples full and sensitised from his unshaven mouth, the rounded weight of her belly and hips tingling with remembered sensuality. The creamy remnants of physical satisfaction

153

glimmered in her dark eyes, in the crushed-petal softness of her mouth.

She was hungrier than she had ever been in her life, ravenous, dying from starvation, parched with desolate thirst and aching with need. For what?

For what, Yvonne?

Where to find what she didn't know she was looking for? It was an impossible task, worthy of rank among the most celebrated of searches throughout literature and history. The knights of the Round Table in their hunt for the Holy Grail, Moses in need of the still, small voice of his God, Macbeth in search of kingship and greatness, Orpheus desperate to find his Eurydice, humanity reaching for the moon.

She dropped her head into her hands. Once she had been lost and in search of herself, but she had that now, indisputably, and it was not enough. Yvonne was not enough.

Naturally the day progressed. Naturally came the time when she was reunited with Adam. All of this was to be expected and not even open for discussion or debate; but what was an intolerable surprise, what rocked her on her feet and sent her head into a giddy, intoxicated fume, was the quality of the experience, the exotic, ascendant, coalesced, sheer driven impact of the man and her reaction to him.

The stress was gone from him. The violence, the compulsive, furious inward gnawing, the harsh severity: he was a slate wiped clean of the strain-induced fissures. He had fractured and come close to some terrible breaking point of stamina and intent, and now, after a night of very little sleep and a marathon bout of physical expenditure, he emerged in a ravishing whole, a prime and incandescent man shimmering with intellect and animal vitality.

She stared upon his golden, handsome face, which was vivid with bright laughter at something Richard had said to him, and she was numb with a solitary, private shock. He was lovely. He was a masterpiece of transcendence. All previous outbursts of temper were forgiven and forgotten. The complex swarmed around him, drawn by the sparkling effervescence, eager to bask in the magnetic glow. Whatever his inner demons had been, he had struggled with them and overcome them; but she—she had demons of her own to battle with, and she was floundering.

She acted the whole, interminable day long. She was Hannah with superiority, even according to her own punishing standards, and when she was not working she was the best projection of Yvonne that she could possibly be: light with an employment of delicate malice that struck infallibly at her intended victims' sense of humour, and never at their vulnerabilities; relentless with a wicked charm that even her opponent Rochelle succumbed to at long last; molten with sultry, sensual laziness; hooded, massive eyes smiling with secretive, unshakeable poise.

She never broke character, never unmasked, not for one single moment. Yes, the shabby performing clown knew how to shuffle.

The end of the day saw the end of Christopher's job. Dinner was a going-away party for him, and all the cast and crew assembled for it, an affectionate and regretful farewell. In warm gratitude her father proposed to host a reunion party for everyone who was returning to Los Angeles after the filming, and his invitation was greeted with uproarious acceptance.

Afterwards, Adam gave Yvonne the keys to his BMW so that she could drive her father to Phoenix Airport; what they talked about for the two hours, she never recalled. She only knew that the trip had been pleasant and undemanding, and that she hugged her father goodbye and told him that she'd see him in Los Angeles in a few weeks' time, and she watched him stroll into the airport terminal with unexplained tears in her eyes and a lump in her throat.

It was ten o'clock in the evening, and she was boneweary. Adam had offered to juggle the next day's schedule so that she wouldn't be needed until later in the morning and she could stop in Phoenix overnight, but with typical self-defeating obstinacy she had refused.

She made the drive back to the location in an hour and a half, breaking the speed limit quite emphatically, pushing fate, the powerful car, her luck. She drove well, and the highway was practically deserted, and there was nary a policeman to harass her. How typical. Sometimes one couldn't find trouble no matter how enthusiastically one looked.

She gentled the BMW's hurtling speed upon reaching the dirt road turn-off, for she didn't want to mark the expensive car, and crept up to the location in a nearly soundless purr. Eleven-thirty was a terribly late hour on a work night when the next day began, as always, at dawn. Aside from a very few floodlights, and one or two windows still profligately shining, the temporary little city was silent.

She left Adam's car in its usual place with the keys in the ignition; there was no fear of anybody stealing it, after all, and she walked to her trailer in a slow stride eloquent with exhaustion, her head bent.

She climbed the steps to the door, and opened it, never noticing that hers was one of the few windows still shining with light. The golden lamp-glow was a fresh and surprising onslaught, as she entered the trailer and found Adam wide awake, engrossed in a newspaper and reclining on her settee.

Sometimes one had a talent for finding trouble when one least expected it.

His auburn head jerked up at her entrance, and her dark gaze and his grey eyes met, in one melded instant of mutual astonishment. He was the quicker to recover, however, as his dark brows plummeted into a harsh frown and he took in the digital display of his wrist-watch, then looked at her in a classic double-take.

'What are you doing here?' he demanded.

She stared at him as he rose off the settee and stalked over to her. 'What an odd question,' she uttered, and threw her bag carelessly on to the table. 'Shouldn't I be asking that of you?'

He was absolutely furious, and she didn't have the energy to face him. He accused, 'You're not supposed to be back for at least another half-hour yet!'

She blinked, feeling sluggish under his attack, and was immensely proud of how her mouth reacted without conscious volition, as she heard herself say in a dry voice, 'If you like, I shall be happy to leave and come back again.'

A tiny muscle moved in his jaw, ominously displayed along the clean line. He growled, 'How fast did you drive, Yvonne?'

'Oh, for heaven's sake,' she snapped wearily, 'I was fast, but I wasn't foolish. Your precious car is safe enough!'

He looked as if she'd punched him in the stomach, then his hands snaked out to fasten on to her shoulders and haul her against him. 'My car?' he repeated, in mild, terrible contrast to the violence of his actions. 'I wait up for you, get worried with the thought of what might have happened when you walk in far too early, and all you can bitch about is my stupid car? Do you really think so little of me?'

Her face paled, her eyes widened; she was already regretting the thoughtless remark, but she cried, 'You're not my keeper and I don't have to account to you for my actions. If you don't want to hear bitchy remarks, then don't attack me the minute I walk into my own door!'

He was frozen, his eyes darkened to pewter with even greater hurt. He said coldly, as his fingers loosened and fell away, 'Of course you're right. Whether you kill yourself or not should be no concern of mine.'

If she was the dark mistress of vicious goading, then he was the master. The sardonic bite of his words sank into her jugular, and she would have shielded herself from him if she could only find out where that vulnerable blind spot was inside her. She squeezed her eyes tight and dug the heels of her hands into them, never one to be extravagant with her tears, especially twice in one day, forcing the weak flood back, back.

'Adam,' she said then, raggedly, 'I'm tired. I'm sorry you feel the need to take your anxieties out on me, I'm sorry you don't approve of how fast I drive, I'm sorry I lost my temper. Most of all I'm sorry because I could have felt happy that you waited up for me, and yet I don't since it's been such a nasty experience. Now, if you're still spoiling for a fight, you'd better just go away, because I'm not in the mood to oblige you.'

He was silent. His silence went on and on. He said quietly, 'I shouldn't have attacked you like that. I was looking forward to seeing you too.'

His rich voice was so gentle that it enticed one of her eyes to make a wary appearance from behind her hand. It considered him thoughtfully. She offered, 'Maybe I shouldn't have gone at eighty. I just wanted to get back.'

'Eighty!' The word burst from him like a bullet, and she winced, and he checked himself abruptly. He gritted his teeth, and said with a smile of severe control, 'You don't want to fight, and I don't want to storm out of here. Let's try something new, shall we? Let's attempt to compromise. You do know what the word means, don't you?'

A little more of her face emerged, a very little grin. His eyes were so gorgeous when they were rueful and smiling like that, and she didn't want him to storm out either. What a horrible let-down to the wonderful surprise of finding him awake, and waiting for her. But she was cautious. She said dubiously, 'It depends. What kind of compromise do you have in mind?'

His stern expression softened, like harsh mountain snows melting, and he brushed away the barrier of her hands as he reached for her face and stroked the hair back from her forehead. He warmed, in face and body and spirit, and shed that warmth all around her, and he bent to kiss her upturned mouth with a light fervency that made her gaze go smoky with delight.

He didn't crash through her defences. He slid through them with sensuous liquidity.

'I promise never to shout at you again when you walk in the door,' he murmured throatily, raining kisses on her, each successive one deeper than the last, harder, a quick, intense, tantalising escalation that stirred the hunger inside her into a consuming blaze. 'I promise instead to meet you in a much more—pleasurable fashion.'

His subsequent halting of the sexual assault was fiercely abrupt. By then she was clinging dazedly to his wrists. His hawkish grey eyes piercing, he murmured just over her trembling mouth, 'Now it's your turn. What do you promise me?'

She whispered, her mind whirling, 'I—I don't know.'

He made a beleaguered sound that whistled through his nostrils, slid his long fingers around her head as if he would like to tear it off her shoulders, and growled, 'You promise never to drive at eighty again.'

Her gaze slowly narrowed, focused on the twisted, elegant mouth that he denied her, and she licked her dry lips and accused him, 'You're manipulating me again.'

'Yes, darling,' he murmured. 'And if I can get that promise from you, I'll not be sorry for it either. Be late for the rest of your life, be late for your own wedding, I don't care—just don't be early for your own funeral, OK?'

He was watching compulsively the circular path of her tongue. It rattled her so badly that she tucked it back inside her mouth and whispered, 'OK.'

His concern had been badly expressed and gracefully retracted; and her speed had been far too high and would never be repeated. Another governance, another check

on her heedless path through life, another adaptation.
If she brought him down with humility, he re-routed her
behaviour with vulnerability. A fair exchange, an
equitable arrangement. She let it go; she had been wrong;
she didn't want to see the hurt in his eyes again or that
shaken expression when she scared him. What did it
matter?

It didn't matter at all. It was wiped away as of monu-
mental unimportance. It was forgotten in a heartbeat
when he showed her how delightful the rewards of
compromise could be, as he kissed her in thanks and
went in search of the tongue she had hidden from him.

And when she moaned at the invasion he groaned his
pleasure, stepping up the heat, stepping back from the
negotiation table, throwing in his chips, raising the
stakes, until too much was at stake for them to stop.

His lead was demanding, imperative. She danced along
after him, knowing now how the song ended, greedy for
the final strains. Several times she thought she was almost
there and threw herself wide open to embrace the
crescendo, but ruthlessly, relentlessly he prolonged the
sexual concert. He would not let her peak.

He was bowed over her splayed body, buried so deep
he thought he might never emerge again. His aggression
had a brilliance of fluctuating rhythm that she couldn't
adjust to, and instead of destroying her anticipation it
brought her to an unbearable sobbing pitch.

Until, at last, shaking and heaving as he bore her
down, glaring wild-eyed up into his poised, intent,
waiting face, she dragged the air into her rasping lungs
and screamed an incoherent demand and plea.

Instantly, before the sound could even break from her
lips and awaken the entire complex, he clamped a hard

hand over her mouth, the heavy thrust of his palm pushing her head into the bed, and her teeth sank into his flesh involuntarily as she shuddered and came with an intensity that threatened to rend her muscles from her bones.

It was too much. She shook and heard the animal sounds that she made. Overwhelmed by what he had done to her, he tried to shush her with tenderness, but, faced with her loss of control, his own snapped in the violent heat of his explosion, and she was the one, after all, to hold him in a welcoming, absorbing embrace as he gave her everything inside him, in racking pleasure, in sudden gushing surrender.

The last weeks.

Camelot's glory had shone so very brightly because its days were numbered. Yvonne knew it.

She knew the reason for the intensity that burned through her translucent skin like a candle. She knew that everyone else saw it, had some dim sense for their awe; she knew that, though she and Adam trod a delicate path between discretion and the refusal to hide, nobody was fooled. The reality of her relationship with the director spread through the complex in some form of osmosis. People just picked it up in a cellular fashion.

Adam made no pretence of disaffection. Quite the opposite, in fact, for he would have been far more physically demonstrative in public except that she stopped him dead with her withdrawal: the imperceptible retreat of her head when he might have kissed her cheek; the remoteness in her eyes when his hand automatically caressed her arm or shoulder; the containment in the disposition of her slender body, the gracefully crossed legs, the narrow hands never left outflung in idle invitation.

She checked his physical expression, but he checked his gut instinct for pursuing the issue, for forcing her to acknowledge him. He bit the whiplash reaction back, and thought a moment or two, and approved. Their entire communication and eventual consensus was reached in silence. They were rewarded for their restraint by at first a wary acceptance from everyone else that gradually became whole-hearted approval and respect, as professional integrity was maintained not by promise, but in actuality.

The daily restraint was a constant recurring battle. She was reminded of the classical scenario in hell, where the unfortunate individuals must push a boulder up a hill; but before attaining the crest the boulder invariably escaped their hold to roll to the bottom, and they had to begin again the eternal, futile task.

Her restraint was greater than his. Her hell was deeper. Hers extended far beyond just the nuances of checking a daytime display of physical affection in public, but was an unceasing twenty-four-hour vigil. Whole areas of conversation were forbidden, entire avenues of extrapolation strangled at birth. Any idle postulations about the future she cut dead, any reference to life outside their carefully cultivated hothouse was reined in with an iron hand. She would not hope, she would not yearn, she would not hypothesise. The universe ended when the filming ended; nothing else existed.

Those were her boundaries. For once in her life she didn't struggle in a snarled tangle but held to her goal with an extraordinary clarity of dry-eyed vision. What would come would come, and would not be considered.

And the nights, oh, the nights. The restraint throughout the day was dry tinder; coming together with Adam in privacy was the lit match. The nights were wild, unbearable, ecstatic, obsessive. She couldn't sleep for the nights. She pretended to eat for his sake, and did ingest enough to maintain. But he was not fooled, for she grew slender as a wraith, a glowing wraith that burned from the inside. She was sustained by her own immense strength, and being destroyed by her indomitable spirit.

Sometimes he tried to stay away, to give her ease, for she needed more rest than he did. She only came after him in a compulsive, fevered rush, and after just a few attempts he no longer bothered, for he was maddened by the daily restraints, victimised by control, rampant, unstoppable.

It was fine. It was another mutual agreement. She welcomed him. Let him break into her at night, a sensual thief come to plunder the willing treasure; for by day she was an unassailable fortress.

Humans inhabited a finite universe of endings. While Adam stayed for the very last scenic shots, Yvonne finished her own work along with the rest of the cast. He had not invited her to stay. She bled at the cut, calm-faced and smilingly.

Their last night together had a keening edge of impending separation to it. After they had made love, Adam talked desultorily about her father's party, to which she listened companionably. He spoke of seeing her in Los Angeles within the week, which was not so long away really, and she was attentive. He happened to casually mention a repeat performance of the hot dogs on the beach, which produced a quick grin, and the entire time she was silent, silent, silent.

Yvonne was one of a general exodus to the airport the next morning. Her farewell to Adam after breakfast was a light-hearted, gaily executed affair, by the cars which were packed and ready to go. She turned away from him, her bland façade impenetrable; they had so many witnesses.

A hand closed around her upper arm, all the way around and then some. He yanked her around so fast that the world spun, hauled her into his arms, and proceeded to ravish her mouth with a long, ferocious, unashamedly passionate, devastatingly thorough kiss. When he finally raised his head, she lay boneless against the hard barrier of his arms and the whole of their goggling audience was beside itself with glee. He considered her stunned eyes and flushed face with a dark, hawkish satisfaction.

'Remember that,' he advised her softly as he let her go.

He swung away; she stumbled back. Maybe somebody caught her. She wasn't sure. All she knew was that she hadn't fallen to the ground because somehow she was sitting beside a whooping Sally in the back of Jerry's car as they drove away.

'Oh, I envy you that one,' gasped the other actress when at last she could speak. 'One of history's greatest kisses with one of the world's sexiest men, and it'll never even make the big screen!'

Yvonne's recovery was white-faced and unamused. She managed a pained smile, for the sake of friendship and politeness, and murmured distractedly, 'Look—do you mind?'

'Oh! Oh, not at all!' Sally exclaimed, quick to sense her unwelcome intrusion. 'You just have to admit it was a hell of a send-off, that's all!'

'Indeed.' Her reply was frozen and unmistakable: the subject was closed for discussion.

She had to bear with convivial company all the interminable way back to Los Angeles Airport. When she waved the last friendly goodbye and sank into the back seat of a taxi, she had come to the end of her endurance.

The ride to her parents' home in Beverly Hills was accomplished in a dreamy haze. Her driver was effusive with his good fortune, elated with the large tip she had given him. He insisted on carrying her luggage inside and asked for her autograph. She gave it to him and waved him off wearily. Betty and her mother Vivian greeted her return with exuberance and informed her she was just in time for lunch.

Yvonne turned on her heel, trudged up the stairs to the suite of rooms that had always been hers since she was a little girl, would always be hers no matter how long she was gone, or how many times she returned, kicked off her shoes and fell fully clothed into her bed and slept until late the next morning.

She was still in a dream when at last she woke up. She was fed well, and she showered, and the afternoon passed, and she had a quiet supper with her parents and listened silently to the plans for the party for cast and crew on Friday evening, and she fell into bed again and slept the clock around.

She spent the next three days like a zombie. Things happened all around her, and she watched them with calm amazement, patting yawns with a languid hand. So much bustling noise, so much vitality. Flowers were ordered, and so was food and drink from the usual caterers—Vivian always used the same company, they were so superb at what they did—and the huge mansion was polished from top to bottom, and the swimming-pool was cleaned, and musicians—they had to have the right musicians. When the Trents threw a party, they did so lavishly; they so loved a good party.

At some point, she knew she would have to wake up. This deadened drifting was getting her nowhere, but she couldn't seem to help it. She had used up too much emotion. She'd blown a fuse and the lights had gone out. She was in perpetual culture-shock with reality; the universe had ended, and the sky had not crashed down around her ears, and life somehow, somewhere was still going on.

Early Friday evening Yvonne sat at the end of her bed. Observing Betty was sometimes like watching a tele-vision with a broken volume control. There was no way to turn her down or tune her out. The maid chattered happily about what Yvonne could wear to the party as she rummaged in the wardrobe—Yvonne saw the machi-nations of her mother in the conversation, and she knew she was being prodded second-hand. She'd worked hard, and had been granted a well-deserved few days' rest, and now it was time to snap out of it.

Adam would have flown in just that afternoon. Their guests were already arriving; he would be along any time now. She finally managed to focus on the fact that she had to get dressed, and she paid attention to the sugges-tions Betty made.

The clothes she had brought from Montana were uni-formly casual, but her wardrobe was stuffed with a history of glittering outfits, products of other occasions

and other parties, all expensive designer labels with an
infantry of matching shoes, most of which hadn't dated
because when she had chosen to dress up she'd preferred
and looked best in classic simplicity.

What to wear? More to the point, what did she want
Adam to see? She wanted him to see nothing, she wanted
to avoid seeing him altogether, she wanted to go to sleep.
She wanted the dream to continue, for she was still in
the avoidance mode. She didn't want to see what the
next step was, if there was a next step, and she didn't
want to take the last step. Her foot was frozen in mid-
air. But a decision had to be made. Betty was rather torn
between a Givenchy and a Chanel.

Yvonne sighed and put her foot down.

Ten minutes later she left a bitterly disappointed maid,
and descended the stairs with light, quick steps. She was
dressed in olive-green fatigues and a sleeveless, skin-tight
matching jersey top. The outfit was relentlessly casual
and unpretentious—why change horses in midstream?—
the colour so muted as to appear drab. She somehow
managed to avoid being washed out, however, for its
dull severity made her tanned skin even more vibrant,
her eyes sparkle with dark brilliance, and brought out
the red and gold highlights of her glossy, unbound
chestnut mane.

She was in good company. Quite a few people were
dressed, her parents among them, but a good portion
of the rough-and-tumble crew were in jeans.

So was Adam.

The sight of him woke her up. He was hard, angled,
his dark head a vintage wine, his hands resting negligently on slim hips. He was the only person in the entire
world, as he stood listening to something Sally said to

him, his handsome face creased with laughter. He was virile, and beautifully relaxed, and scintillating with the minimum of lazy effort, his elegant mouth smiling, his winter-grey eyes bright with amusement. He was a picture of success and unconcern, and a powerful blow to her mid-section. She looked at him, and knew a ferocious empty ache inside her, and an incredulity that she had ever been passionately intimate with those hands, those eyes, that mouth.

As it happened, he was only staying for an hour.

Adam glanced around, caught sight of her, and his face lit up. She discounted the sight without even conscious thought, a living, breathing casualty to too many cooing Hollywood reunions, but when he broke off from talking to Sally in mid-sentence and strode quickly over to wrap her into a tight, rib-cracking hug that had to mean something, didn't it?

'God, it's so good to see you,' he said, his face in her hair and taking a deep breath as if it were the first one in his life. Her arms went around his waist, her head to his shoulder so naturally, so easily—that had to mean something too, didn't it, if only she could figure out what it was...?

And then he was making a mess of the whole thing, throwing her into yet another miserable state of confusion, as she heard him say with leaden regret, 'Maybe I shouldn't have come, but I had to see you even if it was only briefly. Darling, I've got to fly to London tonight—something urgent has come up.'

'Something urgent?' she parroted, her lovely eyes blank.

Adam pulled back and cupped her face in his hands, such a searingly familiar gesture. His gaze was probing, deadly serious, impacting with laser-focused intensity upon her soul.

'Quite a matter of life and death, I think,' he murmured in sober reply, his thumb caressing her lower lip. 'Things should be concluded quickly now, at any rate, and I hope I'll see you soon.'

She listened, because he seemed to be saying something that was vitally important to him, but she wasn't sure she got the point. The brief time he was with them was over in a heartbreaking beat, an eyeblink, and she was left to return to her numb, distant dream.

The numbness came to an excruciating end on Sunday morning. It happened over coffee and a lazy browse through the paper.

Sometimes one's past came back to haunt one. Sometimes one's past came back to haunt other people. Witness Adam's upset at the traumas and disappointments she'd experienced; witness her reaction to the large black and white photograph in the entertainment section, of him in the arms of his whatsit in London.

CHAPTER TEN

YVONNE took one look at the photograph and detonated with a shriek of discovery and rage.

The discovery was because the dreadful shock opened her eyes at last to the truth of how she felt about Adam, and the truth was appallingly huge, more vast than anything she'd ever felt before.

No wonder she'd been so insistent from the earliest point that she wouldn't be changed, she wouldn't make love to him, she wouldn't fall in love. That had been her common sense tapping her on the shoulder and telling her that she'd better beware, or she'd be in over her head before she knew it. Well, she made a hell of prophet, if only she'd taken heed. She'd tripped in massive style, fallen deep and far and flat on her face in love with him.

She loved him—dear God she loved him. Her head said it over and over again in astonished litany. Always known for the longevity of her emotions, an expert at recognising the symptoms, she knew that the suddenness of her realisation had no part in capricious whim but was a stern, bedrock acknowledgement of the consequences of a slow-building disease. She loved him, she was in love with him. The bonding had taken such firm root in her soul that to try to excavate it now would be fatal.

The rage, after that discovery—well, it was self-explanatory. She explained it to herself, practically gnashing her teeth with the violence rocketing through

her. She explained it to her family, all of whom had come
running in terror as her bellow almost blew out all the
windows in the house.

'Look at him!' she shrieked, thrusting the paper
shakily, furiously under Christopher's nose. 'Will you
just look at the bastard?'

Her father took a look, took a second, very hard look,
and became extremely grave. Her mother looked as well.
Then they looked at each other. Her brother didn't even
try to crowd in for a look, but disappeared as soon as
he saw that she hadn't had some debilitating accident.

'Sweetheart,' said her father doubtfully, 'I'm quite sure
that it isn't what it looks like. Adam must have a perfectly good explanation. Just because the Press has
jumped to a few conclusions, it doesn't mean
that——'

'Don't talk rubbish, Christopher!' she snarled, and
threw the paper at her father's chest. 'Of course it's what
it looks like! That isn't some light-hearted, misunderstood embrace—that's the woman he was involved with
a couple of years ago! Damn it, damn the man to hell!
Oh, for God's sake, just go away—yes, I'm all right—
what do you think I am, some shrinking violet or
something?'

Since she had been acting just like one for the last
several days, her parents didn't quite know what to say
to her. They did as she asked; they did as they had always
wisely done whenever she had been in a uncontainable
rage: they left her alone to work her way out of it.

She stood, utterly still, the beating in her blood like
the sonorous clangs of a great bell tolling, like a judge's
gavel coming down in a ringing proclamation of a life
sentence. Then she sprang on the newspaper which had

fallen to the floor and lay submissive like the fluttered wings of a dirty, dying moth.

She spread the paper out, with fingers gentle in extremity and desperation, and commenced upon the first stage of a path of destruction, as she tore out the photograph so carefully, as she held it in shaking hands, staring at what she could see of his face.

Why, Adam? she asked the frozen visage in silence as she knelt on the floor. He had said that he wanted to mark her, and thus publicly proclaim her for his own. Well, he had marked her all right, indelibly, but the marks were invisible ones that she could hide forever if she so wanted; she could play-act for the rest of her life, pretend a recovery, and no one would ever know.

She thought she had come to terms with the possibility of a temporary bonding, with the inevitable break, but she hadn't. She hadn't and she never would.

He had said that he wanted to mark her; he had kissed her in front of so many witnesses, then whispered for her to remember it; he had come to see her for so brief a time on Friday because he could not stay away. Was it all a lie?

No, it had been the truth; her barriers were too sophisticated, too seasoned to allow her to become the dupe to insincerity. And if there was one thing she would have said about Adam, it was that he was not the kind to be fickle; his surface coolness covered a wellspring of emotional intensity that ran too deep for fickleness. Oh, he was a deep one, was the winter king, deep in subtle mystery, a puzzle-box of unexplained, subterranean intent. He had meant what he'd said at the time he'd said it, and now he was in the arms of another woman, one beautiful like the coolness of an English garden.

It was outrageous; it was unthinkable.

She surged to her feet, sprang for the telephone on the bedside table. She made several phone calls: to her agent, to Montana, to the movie studio, to the airlines, to a taxi company. Everyone was so polite and obliging. It was all so ridiculously easy.

Then she razed through the room, a falcon in soaring flight. Her preparations were completed within half an hour. She was packed in twenty minutes. She ran downstairs with her suitcase and went to talk to her father.

Christopher was a calm, patient figure lounging outside by the pool. His eyes were dark with sympathy and pain for her as he watched her walk up to him. She said without preamble, 'I need to get into the safe. I want my passport, and I have my credit cards, but I need some cash. Can I pay you back when I return?'

'Don't be offensive, Yvonne,' he said as he rose to his feet immediately. And with deep, unreserved love, with generosity, without questions or demands for qualifications, he went into his study, opened the safe, and gave her several hundred dollars, and the passport that she'd left behind two years ago along with her former life. 'I don't like the thought of you carrying too much cash around. Is that enough, or do you think you need more?'

'It's more than enough,' she whispered through a tightness in her throat, looking down at the notes in her hand. 'It's always been more than enough.'

She was not talking about the paltry sum of money, and he knew it. He stroked her head and said quietly, 'God bless, darling. In whatever you decide to do.'

Betty came to the door with the news that her taxi had arrived. Yvonne looked up, her eyes far too bright, and said to her father, 'I have to go.'

'Please don't stay away for so long,' her father said carefully, standing very still. Not holding her, never that, for it didn't work with her; just asking. 'We miss you terribly when you're gone.'

'I'll come back,' she said fiercely, and hugged him tight. 'I'll always come back.'

And then she was gone, brightly shot from the nest, and the grounded mortal who had fathered such a trial, such a triumph, watched her passage, with humble gratitude for the privilege of experiencing the miracle of his child, with a heart full of silent shining pride.

She went to ground at Gatwick Airport on Monday morning, and took a taxi into a rain-drizzled London.

She defeated herself, for she had been too wound up to sleep during the long flight, and jet-lag was always worse for an individual suffering from stress. She had to check into a hotel, and was raging at her own limitations even as a black weight descended on her, and she slept like a rock until evening.

Then, vampire-like, her eyes opened in full, deadly alertness. She rose from her bed, calmly showered, and dialled the telephone number the movie studio had been so pleased to provide her with. It rang and rang, and was eventually answered by a British female voice that said politely, 'Adam Ruarke's residence.'

The vitriol wished to spill out of her at the evidence of the woman; she would not let it, not yet. She said very softly, 'Is Adam in?'

'May I ask who's calling?' asked the woman pleasantly.

She had no choice. She would get nowhere otherwise. She told the hated, faceless voice, 'Yvonne Trent.'

The woman warmed immediately, inexplicably. 'Oh, Ms Trent—hello! I'm Adam's housekeeper, Mrs McFaddan. I'm afraid you've just missed him—he's gone out to dinner.'

Go carefully now, carefully. It was easier to speak to the housekeeper with the hate suddenly gone, with a supreme absence of urgency, with precisely employed indifference, 'Oh, he's at dinner, is he? I'm sorry I missed him.'

The housekeeper said quickly, 'Would you care to leave a message where he can reach you?'

'For him to call me back?' she murmured, doubtfully lazy, wanting to scream. 'But won't he be out very late...?'

'Oh, no, Ms Trent!' the housekeeper assured her. 'He's only gone down the street to the Imperial Dragon for some Chinese. I'm sure he'll return very shortly.'

'Ah,' she said with gentle satisfaction. 'Well, thank you, but no, there's no message.'

'Oh, but Ms Trent——' The housekeeper babbled then, in some urgency. The noise was distracting, so Yvonne hung up on her.

She had all the necessary clues. She showered, considering. He liked a good restaurant. A three-course meal with a wine list, an exclusive clientele and a supercilious *maître d'*. Then she dressed, dragged her hair ruthlessly into a chignon, away from her predatory face, and rang down to the hotel lobby and ordered a taxi.

She flowed into the muted, elegant restaurant, the Chanel dress a sleek black silk drape, and she ate the supercilious *maître d'* in one delicate bite. He was overcome with the honour. She allowed him to lead her to a table, a slender feminine tower who was over six feet tall in her heeled pumps, the gracefully muscular legs going up to the sky, a timeless presence with an unforgettable face that left a wake of devastation wherever she passed.

Then she saw them across the way. Adam and the whatsit, together at a candle-lit corner table for two. Yvonne didn't waste more than a glance on the lovely woman. She sank without looking into the chair the *maître d'* held out for her. All of her, all the dark immensity of her eyes and soul, was focused on Adam.

He was a stranger in his formality. He was frightening, in his black suit and white shirt, a stark statement of power like a declaration of mourning or of war. The golden approachable charm was terrible in its absence; his handsome face was harsh and severe and formidable, the grey eyes dull, unignited, transforming the fire in the auburn head from the warmth she remembered to a frostbitten chill. Winter solstice, the death of a year of seasons.

She had discovered, and raged, and come to do battle, pulled by a psychic sorcery, as it were, over thousands of miles. Now that she was here, however, her unquiet spirit come to the audience hall of the winter king, she was faced with his vast enigma and was silenced.

She did nothing. She didn't know what else to do. She crossed her long legs and looked her fill on the intimate scene of the two talking together, and accepted the dagger-thrust, experiencing the killing pain with something almost like serenity.

She didn't have to do anything. The wake of devastation as she had passed through the restaurant was a slow, murmurous time-bomb that did it all for her. The change in atmosphere, the brief quiet of conversation at her entrance; she watched the tidal wave reach the pair, who looked around at the disturbance.

The dead of winter looked upon her, and flared to life.

Flared, blazed, roared out of grey eyes made brilliant by the profligacy of emotion. He made a sudden movement, and whitened, and she heard the tiny sharp tinkle of glass as his wine spilled on to the table and stained the heavy white cloth.

She knew the answer to the enigma then, for the photograph in the newspaper had been true; it was her understanding of it that changed irrevocably.

Her gaze widened with awareness of what he had done, and what she had revealed, with the shielded voltage of communication that ran back and forth along the bond between them, growing exponentially, intensifying in strength, until she sprang from her table with an electrified cry and turned to run from it. He'd given her fair warning that he was a manipulator.

The man she had left behind snapped a few words to his companion, who smiled and nodded in understanding. Then, released, he lunged in an athletic dance through the pattern of tables, so very quick, so precise, that he never touched a stick of furniture or another person.

All Yvonne could think of was escape. She was awfully good at it. She was out of the restaurant, down the dark and yellow-lit street, and around a corner before she even knew it. Gut instinct, knee-jerk reaction. She was panting with the force of her flight and still moving fast, but she couldn't escape the knowledge in her head.

It had all been a set-up. He had set her up. The delicate, far-reaching complexity of it overwhelmed her. The look in the whatsit's eyes: warm, kind, friendly and unsurprised. The ridiculous ease with which she had obtained his London address and phone number from the movie studio. The unexplicable urgency of his housekeeper, who had been all too eager to supply her with information. The photograph published with such alacrity in the Los Angeles newspaper. It had all been patiently choreographed, expertly primed, all arranged with a master touch. It had all led in a tangled weave back to him.

He had tried to speak of future things in Arizona, and she had denied him. She had made herself into an unassailable fortress, and he had set himself out to conquer her. He had not made the futile attempt to storm her unscaleable barriers, but in the classic move of an ingenious strategist had induced her to open the gates and come out. Stunned, reeling, laid irretrievably bare, she covered her shaking mouth and sobbed.

Racing footsteps sounded behind her and came to a precipitate halt. Adam called her name in his fierce hawk's cry, and the exultancy in it, the tortured impending loss, the terror and the ecstasy cut off her escape and bound her to the earth.

She halted, quivering, her back to him, and shouted at her shadow, 'What you did!'

'Oh, God, don't leave.' The raw, hoarse plea broke from him with a power that nearly sent her to her knees.

'I die when you leave. I don't know how many more times I can resurrect myself. Yvonne, what do you know? What do you know now?'

'I won't!' she cried, arms at her sides, hands fisted. I won't bend, I will stand straight, I will break. See how I'm breaking?

'You won't, but you did,' he said, desperate in his ruthlessness. 'You did every time. I compelled, and you fought. I asked, and you gave. I invited, and you came. I left, and you followed. I loved—I love. I love you, Yvonne. I will love you, Yvonne. I will always, always love you; don't kill me with it.'

'You manipulated,' she sobbed, tears streaming from her face, and then her bewildered, proud head lowered. She whispered, 'You won.'

He must have been so close to her, for she heard the harsh struggle of his breathing, the dreadful evidence of a man in mortal danger. He must have been so close as to touch her quaking shoulders, and yet he did not.

'I have not won,' he said. 'I have lost everything to you. You don't even understand how complete your victory is. Oh, you could rival the original doubting Thomas, you could. I don't know how to give you what I need to give you, because you refuse to take it.'

She wrapped her arms around her torso, rocking herself a little in absent solace. 'If I turn around,' she mused, terrified with need, 'if I turn around, you'll vanish. If I reach for you, you'll go away again.'

The silence was grim, dangerous, then he said in shattering warning, 'If you *don't* turn around, I will vanish. If you *don't* reach for me, I'll go away. I'm not made out of stone. I have simply not got an inexhaustible supply of endurance. You extend me beyond my furthest reach, and I am tied to you, and I adore you, and, if you misuse me, I could learn to hate you.'

'We would be parting, always parting—you with your films to make and homes in different countries, I—I with this great big hole inside me that I keep falling into—Oh, God!' she moaned keeningly.

'Have you forgotten so soon the art of compromise?' he murmured in pain. 'I'm going soon. You have to give up your never-never land and make your choice.'

She closed her eyes. She could hear the fissure begin in her, the crack running right through the heart.

The gentle, inexorable voice behind her said, 'I'm going now. Goodbye, Yvonne.'

And then the most amazing thing: she screamed his name in agony and despair from the bottom of her soul, and lost her heart forever, and did not break. She bent at the middle and would have fallen to the ground, would have gone to the lowest point she could possibly go in utter, complete supplication to the winter king, except that he had warned, but he had lied, and he had not moved one single step away from her.

And he caught her before she could tumble too far. He was the safety net over the gaping hole. The impact of his hard arms closing around her body made her shudder and gasp, and twist around to cling to his neck.

He cradled her as close to his long body as he could, and it was not close enough. He jerked back, not gently, and unbuttoned his suit jacket and pulled her into the gap, and that was better. It was better for now; it was enough to hear both their hearts racing in united concert, to stroke the dampened hair at her temple, to know a secretive triumph at the trembling of her body, and the fierce exultation at how she had reduced herself to such a point, which only he could save her from.

'Woman, you're a hard learner,' he growled, nuzzling her face.

'I'm a hard learner, because it's forever when I learn it,' she groaned, pushing him back with her nose, urging him to something. 'Adam, I love you. There I've said it now, and I'll not say it again.'

He hesitated. 'You'll not?'

He'd stolen away every gauntlet she had ever thrown down, and she had cast down so many that she was in danger of running out of them. A hard learner could also be a quick study. She said very fast, 'I'll say it every day, thousands of times a day. You'll get sick of hearing it, I'll say it so much, and then you'll tell me to shut up. I just know you will.'

He convulsed against her, laughing so hard he had to lay his head on her shoulder; at least she thought he was laughing, hoped he was. She was worried, in fact, that he might not be, for the racking shudders were an awful struggle. She pulled back to search his face, poised to soothe, to castigate herself for driving them both to such a level, and saw that his lovely grey eyes were filled with tears and dancing with merriment.

He was so vividly alive with expression and emotion, such a startling and complete contrast to the deadened winter from before that the last of her lingering fear blew away, never to return again, for the learner gained a new lesson as she realised that if she had reduced him she had exalted him as well. She brought him beyond his limits, she extended his endurance, and she made him more of a man than he was before.

It was a glorious power she held. She tested it, whispering, 'I love you.'

She watched him ignite with sheerest joy. He whispered back, 'Every time you tell me will be a priceless gift. Every time I hear it will be like new. I will never tire of hearing it, and never stop telling you how much I love you.'

'You'd better not,' she told him with a new-found composure that disintegrated as his face flushed dark, and he ran his hands down the length of her back to grasp at her hips and pull her tight to his.

'Feel what you do to me when you say that you love me,' he said hoarsely, his eyes glittering with fever. 'Be niggardly with your trust, my love, put me to the test. Say it, and reach out with your beautiful hands and feel me.'

It was a hard evidence that he offered her, hard, urgent, pulsing through the constricting material of their clothing. She was frozen against his rampant aggression, her eyes locked with his in startled enquiry.

He groaned and threw a wild glance around the deserted neighbourhood street, then he grasped her hand and pivoted on one heel to stride with escalating speed back around the street corner. Her long legs flashed as she worked to keep up with him; she stumbled on the uneven pavement, and he grimaced, and caught her, and urged her into a run, muttering, 'Hurry, damn it.'

'Adam!' she gasped, in protest at his manhandling.

He stopped for a whirling instant, hauled her to him, and kissed her with unsteady, uncalculated, unskilled ferocity, piercing her smooth chignon with destructive fingers, dragging her hair out of the confinement until it flowed all around her head and shoulders in a dusky, untamed cloud.

He gritted against her parted lips, 'It's been seven long, hard, dry, suspenseful days, and I'm so famished for you that I'll probably take you here in the street if you don't expend a little more effort and start hustling, woman.'

She got the point, and nodded, and hustled. Since his flat was so close by, he hadn't driven to the restaurant, and by the time he dragged her up the garden path and unlocked the door of his ground floor flat she was gasping and dishevelled. She would have laughed if she hadn't caught his urgent need and become a willing accomplice to the seriousness of the intent.

Yvonne wanted to scream at the unexpected intrusion as a matronly figure hurried into the shadowed hall in response to the grating of his key in the lock. 'Mr Ruarke!' puffed the middle-aged woman. 'I'm so sorry— Ms Trent called just as you hoped she would, and I did manage to tell her where you were, but she wouldn't leave a message——'

The housekeeper hadn't caught sight of her yet. Yvonne hung back slyly. 'Thank you for minding the phone, Mrs McFaddan,' said Adam in a serene voice, as his fingers crushed hers to a numb bloodlessness. 'And well done. You did just exactly what you should have done, and now you may go home.'

'Hello, Mrs McFaddan,' said Yvonne as she peeped around the bulk of Adam's shoulder, startling the other woman into a gasp of delight. 'We spoke earlier. How nice to meet you; goodnight.'

'Ms Trent! You're actually here in Britain?' The housekeeper's eyes glowed. 'Oh, it's such a pleasure to meet you! I *love* your films...'

Adam exploded. He forcibly hustled the housekeeper to the front door, talking the entire time. His relentless politeness overrode her astonished squawks. Then he advised her to take the next day off, shoved her out of the door, slammed and locked it. Yvonne leaned her aching head against the wall and laughed until tears streamed down her face.

He didn't turn to her. He planted his fists into the door with a great wooden boom, and gritted, 'Damn— Yvonne, I have no patience left——'

That was the last of it, spent in considerate warning. She licked her lips, looking at his bowed head and hunched shoulders. Control was such an erotic thing to misplace. She helped to bury his, and whispered, 'Adam, I'm so wet.'

He growled, and turned to lunge at her. She fell giddily under his onslaught; he caught her and lowered her gently to the floor. Then that was the last of his carefulness as well. He didn't even bother undressing her, but lifted up her skirt and moved between her legs, unbuckling his trousers, shaking, fumbling, heedless.

It was the most moving and touching thing she had ever experienced, the animal need to couple with this intelligent and humane man. She was helpless before his sensual finesse, and unbearably excited by his consummate patience, but this rough, immense penetration—this she gloried in—again, again, again. And then he propped himself on one elbow to stare down at her, appalled, in wonder, triumphant, and he cried out from the very heart of him, 'I love you!'

She drew him in, all of him, all of the gift, and cried it back, and it was new.

They came home together. They came together, such a long, long way.

The truth and a final understanding.

Said the wife, peaceably, to her husband, 'I told you so.'

Said the husband to his rose-pruning wife, 'You're always right. It isn't fair. Admit it—you had some doubts there, for a little while.'

The wife was a serene and subtle matriarch, hatted and gloved to protect her fine skin from the sun, a delicate queen of the perpetual summer. She gave her husband a secretive smile; that always maddened him.

'I never doubted for a moment,' said the wife, snipping and pruning with great energy, stepping back now and then to consider the loveliness of her design. 'I saw from the beginning that Adam and Yvonne were right for each other. Yin and yang, two halves of a coin. She warms him up, and he draws her out. They'll drive each other crazy for the rest of their lives and love every minute of it.'

The husband considered that, broodingly, then nodded his resignation. 'She thinks I did it,' he said darkly, and began to laugh all over again. 'She thinks I had the entire thing mapped out. I quite like being the recipient of so much respect.'

The wife tapped him on the arm to remind him of his place. 'Don't let it go to your head,' she advised him in a sweet voice.

The husband considered that as well, and sighed. 'Won't you ever tell her that it was all your idea?'

The wife laughed. 'And give up my one advantage of secrecy? Not likely. Now, how do we go about convincing them that they want a great gaggle of children? I can't wait to become a grandmother.'

'I love you,' said the adoring husband to his wife.

She was so busy. She snipped and said happily, 'I know.'

The next Oscar awards ceremony was the first in six years that the famous director Adam Ruarke missed. He triumphed *in absentia*; he and his wife had another pressing engagement.

The labour-room was modern, homey. There was a television they could watch in between her contractions. Yvonne laughed with glee at each award their film won and then groaned in pain successively. Adam told her she sounded like a bizarre kind of mule. She threatened to have him evicted.

The engagement became even more pressing. Yvonne never got to see the part when she won her own Oscar for her portrayal of Hannah. As she was wheeled into the delivery-room, she was shouting furiously, 'I've changed my mind, damn it! Give me drugs, hit me over the head, for God's sake, just take the baby out!'

Adam was overcome, with laughter, worry, terrible empathy, bottomless remorse, heart-shaking excitement. There was only just so much emotion that one man could stand.

He managed admirably, after all; he rose to the occasion; if there was too much emotion, why, he just had to grow to contain it.

His calm, steady coaching was an unfaltering anchor for her to hold on to. She gritted, and poured with sweat, and pushed, and cried that she must be the fattest, ugliest woman on earth, and that he must hate her for it; and he crooned, and supported her straining shoulders, and reminded her to breathe, and said that she was the most beautiful woman he had ever seen, and that he loved her quite terribly, and that they must never make love again.

At that she nearly split her swollen sides with laughing, until the last great contraction squeezed her like a vice, and she screamed ear-splittingly, and gave birth to a tiny, funny-looking, vastly surprised little creature whom she loved at once so much that she burst into noisy tears. The healthy baby girl immediately wailed in concert; a grinning nurse wiped and weighed and measured quickly, then thrust the minute bundle of outrage into her father's stunned arms.

Adam looked from his wailing daughter to his weeping wife. Oh, my God, he had two of them now.

He was quite certain that he was the luckiest man on earth.

4 FREE

Romances and 2 FREE gifts just for you!

You can enjoy all the heartwarming emotion of true love for FREE! Discover the heartbreak and happiness, the emotion and the tenderness of the modern relationships in Mills & Boon Romances.

We'll send you 4 Romances as a special offer from Mills & Boon Reader Service, along with the opportunity to have 6 captivating new Romances delivered to your door each month.

Claim your FREE books and gifts overleaf...

An irresistible offer from Mills & Boon

Become a regular reader of Romances with Mills & Boon Reader Service and we'll welcome you with 4 books, a CUDDLY TEDDY and a special MYSTERY GIFT all absolutely FREE.

And then look forward to receiving 6 brand new Romances each month, delivered to your door hot off the presses, postage and packing FREE! Plus our free Newsletter featuring author news, competitions, special offers and much more.

This invitation comes with no strings attached. You may cancel or suspend your subscription at any time, and still keep your free books and gifts.

It's so easy. Send no money now. Simply fill in the coupon below and post it to -
Reader Service, FREEPOST, PO Box 236, Croydon, Surrey CR9 9EL.

– – – – – – – NO STAMP REQUIRED – – – – – – –

Free Books Coupon

Yes! Please rush me 4 FREE Romances and 2 FREE gifts! Please also reserve mc a Reader Service subscription. If I decide to subscribe I can look forward to receiving 6 brand new Romances for just £11.40 each month, postage and packing FREE. If I decide not to subscribe I shall write to you within 10 days - I can keep the free books and gifts whatever I choose. I may cancel or suspend my subscription at any time. I am over 18 years of age.

Ms/Mrs/Miss/Mr _____ EP71R

Address _____

_____

Postcode _____ Signature _____

Offers closes 31st October 1994. The right is reserved to refuse an application and change the terms of this offer. One application per household. Offer not available for current subscribers to Mills & Boon Romances. Offer only valid in UK and Eire. Overseas readers please write for details. Southern Africa write to IBS Private Bag X3010, Randburg 2125. You may be mailed with offers from other reputable companies as a result of this application. Please tick box if you would prefer not to receive such offers. ☐

mps
MAILING
PREFERENCE
SERVICE

JANET DAILEY

A Collection

Three sensuous love stories from a world-class
author, bound together in one beautiful volume—
A Collection offers a unique chance for new fans to
sample some of Janet Dailey's earlier works and for
longtime readers to collect an edition to treasure.

Featuring:

THE IVORY CANE
REILLY'S WOMAN
STRANGE BEDFELLOW

Available from May   Priced £4.99

WORLDWIDE

*Available from WH Smith, John Menzies, Volume One, Forbuoys, Martins,
Woolworths, Tesco, Asda, Safeway and other paperback stockists.
Also available from Worldwide Reader Service, FREEPOST,
PO Box 236, Croydon, Surrey CR9 9EL. (UK Postage & Packing free)*

HEARTS OF FIRE

By Miranda Lee

HEARTS OF FIRE by Miranda Lee is a totally compelling six-part saga set in Australia's glamorous but cut-throat world of gem dealing.

Discover the passion, scandal, sin and finally the hope that exists between two fabulously rich families. You'll be hooked from the very first page…

Each of the six novels in this series features a gripping romance. And the first title **SEDUCTION AND SACRIFICE** can be yours absolutely FREE! You can also reserve the remaining five novels in this exciting series from Reader Service, delivered to your door for £2.50 each. And remember postage and packing is FREE!

MILLS & BOON READER SERVICE, FREEPOST, P.O. BOX 236, CROYDON CR9 9EL. TEL: 081-684 2141

YES! Please send me my FREE book (part 1 in the Hearts of Fire series) and reserve me a subscription for the remaining 5 books in the series. I understand that you will send me one book each month and invoice me £2.50 each month.

NO STAMP NEEDED

MILLS & BOON READER SERVICE, FREEPOST, P.O. BOX 236, CROYDON CR9 9EL. TEL: 081-684 2141

Ms/Mrs/Miss/Mr: _____   EPHOF

Address _____

_____

_____   Postcode _____

Offer expires 31st. August 1994. One per household. The right is reserved to refuse an application and change the terms of this offer. Offer applies to U.K. and Eire only. Readers overseas please send for details. Southern Africa write to : IBS Private Bag X3010, Randburg 2125. You may be mailed with offers from other reputable companies as a result of this application. If you would prefer not to receive such offers please tick box. ☐

mps MAILING PREFERENCE SERVICE